"I've d ... , Sara...

The sil... against
her pal... ...l her little
finger, ...into his mouth and
sucked.

A languorous heat began deep in her belly. She
watched him in silence, her heart thudding and
prancing as he kissed his way across her wrist
and up her arm.

She caught her breath, closed her eyes and let
a soft, purring sound roll from her throat. She
felt herself tipping back against fresh-scented
pillows as he mouthed a tingling path to the top
of her arm.

He surprised her by licking the tender curve
between her arm and breast.

She cried out at the erotic pleasure, but he had
already shifted; now he nipped at the round crest
of her shoulder. She sighed breathlessly.

"Say it again," he whispered against her ear.

"W-what?"

He gazed heatedly at her mouth. "Say, 'ahhh.'"

Dear Reader,

Being a "people" person, I find the most interesting places to live are small towns, where everyone knows everyone. This could be both a joy and a challenge.

Imagine a handsome, virile, single young doctor in a small town. He would unavoidably come to know most of his patients on a personal basis. He'd be a matrimonial catch. His examination room might be inundated with hopeful lady patients, while other women might be embarrassed going to him with medical problems. His professional bedside manner would play an important role in easing awkward situations. He'd have to be very careful not to blur the line between private and professional relationships.

What if one particular patient, though, makes his pulse race, his temperature rise and his idea of happiness change in a way no other woman ever has? What if she goes to extreme lengths to avoid him on a social basis? Ethically speaking, his hands would be tied.

Hope you enjoy *Say "Ahhh..."* the first book of the BEDSIDE MANNERS series. Be sure to look for my next book in the same series, *Temperature's Rising*, available in July.

Happy reading!

Donna Sterling

SAY "AHHH..."
Donna Sterling

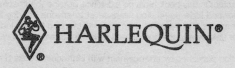

TORONTO • NEW YORK • LONDON
AMSTERDAM • PARIS • SYDNEY • HAMBURG
STOCKHOLM • ATHENS • TOKYO • MILAN • MADRID
PRAGUE • WARSAW • BUDAPEST • AUCKLAND

To the beautiful and gracious Antoinette Reddinger, who told me lively stories from her rocking chair, baked the world's best goodies and always speaks with pride of her four daughters and sons-in-law, twenty-one grandchildren and steadily increasing count of great-grandchildren. We love you, Gram.

ISBN 0-373-25826-7

SAY "AHHH..."

Copyright © 1999 by Donna Fejes.

This edition published by arrangement with Harlequin Books S.A.

® and TM are trademarks of the publisher. Trademarks indicated with ® are registered in the United States Patent and Trademark Office, the Canadian Trade Marks Office and in other countries.

Printed in U.S.A.

1

ALONE IN THE WAITING room of the only medical office in Sugar Falls, Colorado, Sarah stared in dry-mouthed dismay at the New Patient Form. She should have expected this, she supposed. She should have prepared herself for the medical history questions.

The very first one stumped her. "Name."

She felt fairly certain that her first name was Sarah. It had come to her shortly after she'd opened her eyes in the Denver hospital six weeks ago. When her terror at finding her memory a blank had lessened and she'd had time to think, she'd invented a last name. Inspired by a bouquet on her bedside table, she'd become "Sarah Flowers." The emergency-room doctors had believed her when she swore her memory had returned.

Only a single memory had returned, though—a vague, shadowy one that had frightened and confused her.

She knew she should tell this new doctor the truth about her amnesia. But what if word leaked out into this small, close-knit community? Apprehension chilled her. The risk was simply too great to confide in any stranger.

With a heavy heart, she printed "Sarah Flowers."

From there, the questions only got worse. Odd, how she could agonize over questions all night, every night, but feel so devastated just because they were now asked in print. "Age." How could she possibly know? She guessed around twenty-four or -five.

"Birth Date." She chose a month, counted back the appropriate number of years, and wrote down a date.

"Marital Status." She assumed single. She didn't feel married, and she hadn't been wearing a wedding band when she'd been struck by the car. Then again, she couldn't be sure of anything about herself. Did she have a husband waiting for her somewhere? If so, why hadn't he reported her disappearance?

Every new question on the medical form prompted dozens of her own. When she reached the part about pregnancy, her hand trembled so badly she had to set the pen down. Had she ever been pregnant? Had she ever given birth?

Absurd that she didn't know these things about herself! She had to face the fact that she could actually be a mother, with children waiting for her somewhere. The idea of little ones longing for their mother tore at her heart.

The time had come to find answers to all these questions. For six weeks, she'd been stymied by her injuries, her lack of money and her fear inspired by the one dark memory that haunted her. But her injuries were nearly healed now, her new job would provide her with a little money, and her fear no longer had the power to immobilize her.

The only thing stopping her from actively

searching for clues to her past was the dizziness she'd been experiencing lately. She'd come to the doctor to put an end to those vexing dizzy spells. They were sapping her strength and interfering with her work.

Hurriedly she scribbled in fictitious answers on the form and handed it to the receptionist.

"Miss Flowers?" A gray-haired nurse with a kind smile beckoned her into a back room, ushered her onto a scale and introduced herself as Gladys. "The doctor will be a while. He's putting a cast on Danny Harrison's arm." Taking a clipboard from a counter, Gladys recorded her weight. "Now let's see." She peered at the form. "What have you come in for?"

"I was in an accident about six weeks ago. I wanted to make sure my injuries are healing okay." The nurse nodded, wrote something down and stuck a thermometer in her mouth. When she removed it, Sarah added, "I've also had a couple dizzy spells, and I've been feeling more fatigued than usual."

"Sounds like you need a physical." She clamped a blood-pressure cuff on her arm. "We like to start our new patients off with a complete workup, anyway. Any chance you're pregnant?"

Pregnant? Now? She certainly hoped not! She'd been having dizzy spells, yes, and feeling unusually fatigued...and hadn't had a period for at least six weeks—since the accident or possibly longer. But many women missed periods because of physical trauma...didn't they?

"I don't think I'm pregnant," Sarah replied,

stunned by the possibility, "but I'm not really sure."

"We can get that out of the way before the doctor comes in." Gladys removed the blood-pressure cuff and recorded the results. "It doesn't take but a minute to run the test."

Sarah gave the nurse a specimen, then waited in an examination room for the results, gripping her hands in her lap as anxiety knotted her stomach and emotions warred in her chest. She might be carrying a baby! How could she afford to raise it? She worked as a housemaid for little more than her room and board, with only one newfound friend as an ally.

Yet, as panic pressed in around her, the idea of motherhood glimmered with irrational appeal. She might be carrying a baby of her very own! A baby to fill her arms, her heart, her life.

How selfish it was of her, hoping for a baby to relieve her own loneliness. She had nothing to offer a child—not even an authentic last name.

An eternity passed before the nurse returned to the spacious, immaculate examination room. "I don't know if you'll be glad of this news or not, dear," she said in the gentlest of tones, "but the results were negative. You're not pregnant."

Relief swept through Sarah; and yet, a stubborn wistfulness turned her smile bittersweet. *Someday*, she told herself. Someday, when she'd figured out where she belonged, she'd have the luxury of rejoicing in a positive result. For now, she'd have to be grateful for a negative one. "Thank you."

It occurred to her then that the answer to other important questions might be obtained here just as easily. How much information could be gleaned from a physical examination?

"When a doctor performs a physical," she inquired, "can he determine whether a woman has ever had a baby?"

"Usually," Gladys answered rather absently as she prepared equipment on a tray. "There'd be signs."

Sarah pressed a hand to her thumping heart. She could know the answer to that important question, and maybe others, in a matter of minutes! "I'd like the doctor to tell me *everything* he finds out about me," she instructed. "Everything."

Gladys glanced at her, looking dumbfounded. "Like what?"

"Well, like whether I've ever had a baby, or—" Sarah halted, realizing how absurd the request must seem. No wonder the nurse was studying her as if she'd lost her mind. She'd have to explain about the amnesia now, or think of a reason she wouldn't know this very basic fact.

While Sarah struggled with her fear of confiding too much information, Gladys scribbled something on her chart. "You've left the pregnancy section blank," she observed.

A knock at the door saved Sarah from having to reply. A feminine voice called out, "Gladys, you have a call on line two."

Gladys opened the door and conferred with a pretty blonde whom Sarah instantly recognized—a frequent guest at her employer's home. She apparently worked in this office, which meant she'd have access to the files. The entire town, including her employer, could know Sarah's private business by lunchtime!

She ducked her head and let her long, dark hair sweep down to shadow her face, hoping the woman wouldn't notice her. She'd been crazy to even consider mentioning her amnesia.

"Take off all your clothes, hon, and change into one of those gowns over there," Gladys called over her shoulder before leaving to take her phone call. "The doctor will be right in."

Sarah thanked her lucky stars that she hadn't told Gladys more. Obediently she removed her clothes, draped the paper gown over herself and sat on the examination table, trying to figure out a way to ask her questions without having to admit to the amnesia. Maybe she could casually pry information out of the doctor during the exam with a friendly challenge. "Hey, Doc, let's see if you can guess how many babies I've had..."

The door opened and a man walked in.

Sarah's heart paused in surprise. This wasn't the sweet, old grandfatherly doctor her friend Annie had described.

This tall, broad-shouldered man with an athletic build had to be in his early thirties. His dark, vibrant tan contrasted sharply with his white lab coat. Thick, close-cropped hair gleamed maple-golden around his rugged face. He moved with a masculine grace that brought to mind cowboys or gunslingers. Certainly not doctors. Beneath his lab coat, he wore faded jeans and soft leather boots.

He paused a short distance from Sarah and his keen, hazel-eyed gaze locked with hers. For a moment, he said nothing at all, as if the sight of her somehow surprised him.

Why, she wondered, did *he* seem surprised? She was the one flabbergasted. The room grew several degrees hotter—maybe from the potent virility that radiated from him like the sun's rays.

"I'm Dr. Connor Wade." His deep, brandy-smooth voice with its sensual afterburn sent heat spiraling down to her very core. Though he didn't smile, he sauntered closer and extended a large, bronzed hand. "You must be Sarah."

She nodded mutely and shook his hand. It felt warm, callused and unquestionably strong. Though she couldn't remember a single person from her past, she knew she'd never met a sexier, more handsome man in her life.

He released her hand, and she immediately felt bereft, and shaken, and highly conscious of the fact that she sat here on his examination table clad in only a thin paper gown, with not a stitch of clothing underneath.

"Where's Dr. Brenkowski?" she managed to ask, instinctively folding her arms around herself, her fingers splaying across her upper arms. Annie had *promised* her old Doc Brenkowski!

"In Europe. I'm seeing both his patients and mine. You're not a regular patient of his, though, are you?"

"No."

He cocked a brow. She offered no explanation for her question. He glanced at the clipboard he was carrying. Her medical form, she realized. A slight frown drew his tawny eyebrows together, but when he looked back up, the frown was gone.

He leveled her a professional, courteous smile that in no way should have affected her pulse rate.

It did, though. And the air between them seemed electrically charged.

"Gladys wrote that you were in an accident. A bad one?"

"Not too bad," she replied cautiously, watching as he chose a scope from a rack on the wall. She hoped he wouldn't request charts from her previous doctor. She'd written in a false name and address in that section of the form.

He slipped a few medical implements into his lab coat pocket and approached her. "What injuries did you sustain?"

"Broken ribs, bruises, a slight fracture in my right hip—" she faltered as he neared, his gaze sweeping across her in a thoroughly impersonal way "—and a mild concussion."

"Did you lose consciousness?" He stood directly beside her now, which somehow interfered with her breathing.

"Briefly."

"Any memory loss?"

Her muscles clenched. "No."

He glanced at her in mild surprise. "None at all? You mean, you remember the accident itself?"

"For the most part."

"Good." He clicked on the light of a small scope, swept her hair behind her left ear and bent closer. "Did it happen here in Sugar Falls?"

The warmth of the light in her ear and the feel of his fingers in her hair sent a tingling reaction through her. "Pardon me?"

"The accident." He let her hair swing back over

her ear and moved to her other side. "Did it take place here in Sugar Falls?"

"Oh. No. No, it didn't."

He examined her right ear, his breath momentarily warming it, then with an easy touch to her jaw, turned her face from side to side. "I didn't think so. Hadn't heard of any accidents here with injuries in a while. Look straight ahead."

She obeyed, and he trained the light first on one eye, then the other. His ruggedly masculine face was very near, and the scent of a summer forest emanated from his clean-shaven jaw.

Ridiculous, how his nearness sped up her heart!

He clicked off the scope light, slipped the instrument into the pocket of his lab coat, then reached to gently probe with his fingertips the valley beneath her ears and the tender underside of her jaw. Though his manner was impeccably professional, her reaction was much too personal. His scent, his nearness, his touch, all infused her with a keen sensual awareness.

"Are they giving you problems?"

Her startled gaze locked with his. "Th-they?"

"Your injuries." His voice had taken on a husky quality, it seemed, and his fingers stilled at either side of her face.

"Some."

Amusement warmed his hazel eyes to an almost-golden hue. "Do you always talk this much?"

"Never," she breathed.

Their gazes held for a long, dizzying moment. His gentle amusement faded, and the connection between them flared to an odd intensity. His eyes slowly lowered to her mouth.

Her heart drummed.

He grazed her chin with his thumb, and in a near whisper, ordered, "Say 'Ahhh.'"

She merely stared at him. The sensuality coursing through her had distracted her beyond bearing and depleted her voice. She felt a flush rise up her neck into her face.

"It's easier to check your throat," he explained gruffly, "with your mouth open."

She glanced away from him to get a grip on her composure. What was wrong with her? He was behaving exactly as he should, but every move he made stimulated sensual responses in her. Worse yet, she couldn't forget that she was naked beneath this paper gown, and that soon, the exam would become more intimate.

Her arms tightened in a protective self-hug.

"Maybe I should take a look at your injuries," he suggested, "before we continue with the exam." She nodded, and he asked, "Which ones are still bothering you?"

It took an effort to speak, and her voice emerged with a throaty resonance. "My ribs ache at times, and my right hip...well..." Avoiding his gaze, she laid her fingers alongside the curve of her hip as she hesitantly explained, "The place where I injured it isn't bothering me, actually, but there's a strip of numbness running down from it and along my thigh. From about here—" she traced the path with her hand "—to about here."

When he didn't immediately reply, she stole a glance at him. He was staring at her in an intense but unreadable way. Without a word to her, he leaned toward the wall and pushed an intercom button. "Gladys, I need you in room B. *Now*." After an awkward moment, he uttered by way of explanation, "Routine procedure. She helps with all exams."

Sarah suspected it had more to do with the sexually charged tension she couldn't quite hide. Oddly enough, the idea of having a nurse with them in no way lessened that tension.

The doctor seemed somewhat tense himself, his color high beneath his tan and his lips a firm, straight line. Quietly he ordered, "Tell me about your dizzy spells."

She did, and he asked about her medications and diet.

"The dizziness may be from the altitude change," he said. "You've recently moved here from Denver, right?"

Tensing at the question, she nodded. She'd written Denver on her form because she'd known a few street names there.

"We're at a lot higher altitude here. Most people need some time to adjust...some more than others." He went on to talk about how dehydration sets in quicker and how more fluids are necessary.

While he talked, she noticed that his tawny hair lay in thick, neat layers that would probably feel like plush velvet beneath her fingers. The impulse to touch his hair, run her hands against its nap, made her mouth go dry.

Why did he affect her so strongly? Everything about him struck her as hypnotically attractive, from his golden-green eyes to the raspy feel of his hands on her skin.

She realized he'd stopped talking and was simply watching her. Before she could stop herself, words slipped from her mouth without any forethought at all. "Your hands," she mused. "They're callused. I wouldn't expect that in a doctor."

He glanced down at his palms as if he'd never noticed the calluses before. "Must be from rock climbing. Fishing. Horseback riding." He lifted one broad shoulder in a negligent shrug. "Yard work." A slight smile curved one side of his mouth and deepened a vertical crease beside it. She swore her heart contracted. He tilted his head and studied her with even closer attention than before. "Do they bother you—" he asked "—the calluses?"

"Oh...no." Her reply sounded almost dreamy, and she wanted to kick herself. She shouldn't be noticing things like the hardness of his hands, or the silkiness of his hair, or the muscled breadth of his shoulders.

He'd fallen silent, she realized, and so had she. They were again staring at one another with that disconcerting tension growing all the stronger.

"About the exam," he finally said, his voice low and gravelly. "What did you mean when you told Gladys you wanted to know everything I found?"

Sarah swallowed hard against a throat that had gone bone-dry. She'd almost forgotten about the request she'd made to his nurse. Not a single explanation came to mind.

"I believe you asked if I could tell whether or not you've given birth. Care to explain that question?"

Nervously she tossed her heavy hair over one

shoulder and fixed her gaze on the far wall. "I was asking in a general way, just out of curiosity, whether it was scientifically possible for a doctor to tell if a woman had given birth. I didn't mean *me*, specifically."

"Ah. I see." After a reflective pause, he went on, "Then, for the sake of your medical chart, maybe you can fill in the blanks." He loomed nearer, into her line of peripheral vision, his gaze blatantly probing now. "Have you ever given birth?"

Her gaze whipped back to his as she realized her mistake. She couldn't possibly answer him. He'd know soon enough whether or not she was lying. He'd know from the exam more about her physical history than she would, unless he told her. And she wanted so badly to know whatever information could be gleaned.

The gray-haired nurse bustled in, murmuring apologies for being late. Dr. Wade didn't so much as glance at her. His attention was focused entirely on Sarah as he awaited her reply.

"I've changed my mind about the exam," Sarah declared, conscious of her blazing face and the hitch in her voice. "I'd rather wait until Dr. Brenkowski returns."

Dr. Wade stared at her in surprise.

His nurse looked more surprised than he did. "I can assure you, Miss Flowers, that Dr. Wade is one of the finest doctors I've ever worked with," she proclaimed. "He graduated at the top of his class from Harvard, and worked in a busy Boston hospital before he—"

"Gladys, it's okay." He touched her arm to stop her, but kept his gaze trained solely on Sarah. "It's your prerogative, of course, Ms. Flowers, to see whichever doctor you want. And Doc Brenkowski's a good one. But I have to warn you, he won't be back for another month or so."

A month! How could she wait that long to get an answer to such an important question? On the other hand, she couldn't bring herself to allow this vitally handsome young doctor with his heart-stopping stare to examine her so intimately...or to learn that she knew nothing about herself. "A month will be fine," she heard herself assure him.

The nurse looked ready to defend her beloved Dr. Wade again. He himself, however, looked inexplicably relieved. Relieved! Had he expected her to cause him some kind of trouble?

"At the very least, I should take a look at your injuries," he offered, "to make sure there's not something interfering with the healing process. I'd also like to run tests regarding those dizzy spells."

"Actually, my injuries aren't bothering me all that much," she demurred. "And the dizzy spells—"

"Could be dangerous." He rested his knuckles against his hips, and a muscle flexed in his squared jaw. "This is where I have to insist. If Dr. Brenkowski is your physician, then I'm standing in for him right now, and I'm telling you that you need tests. The dizziness is probably caused by the altitude change, but I want to make sure. You also need bed rest—at least a couple days of it. You're showing signs of physical exhaustion."

"Exhaustion!" She hadn't expected that, even though she hadn't been sleeping well and her workload had been strenuous.

"You *are* going to cooperate, Ms. Flowers, aren't you?"

He looked so determined to have his way that Sarah had to smile. "Yes, of course, Dr. Wade. I really wasn't doubting your medical expertise, you know."

It took a moment, but his stern expression finally mellowed, although only a little. His gaze swept across her mouth, her smile. Without offering a smile in reply, he uttered almost inaudibly, "I never thought you were."

DR. CONNOR WADE SHUT the door of his office, dropped down into the chair behind his desk and released a long, tortured breath. He felt as if he'd just gone ten rounds with a heavyweight.

What the hell had happened to him in there?

Whatever it was, it had never happened before. He'd treated plenty of young, beautiful women over the years and hadn't once felt anything more than a professional interest. This time, though, when he entered his examination room and saw Sarah Flowers sitting there, the appointment had gotten off on entirely the wrong track.

He'd known he was in trouble the moment his gaze had met hers. Something about her had stirred him in a deeply personal way. *He'd wanted to touch her.* And after he had touched her, he'd wanted to keep on touching her....

He shut his eyes, leaned his forehead against his clasped fists and cursed himself. Had she sensed his interest? Was that why she'd asked for Doc Brenkowski? Whatever the reason, he was glad that she had. If she hadn't, he probably would have stopped the exam himself.

Probably. He honestly couldn't be sure of that, though.... Which scared the hell out of him.

Why had she affected him so strongly?

Oh, she was beautiful, all right, with her heavy cloud of silky dark hair falling past her shoulders, her creamy complexion begging to be touched, and her wide, silver-gray eyes seeming to look clear through to his soul. But physical beauty had never been enough to elicit more than a brief acknowledgement from him before—at least, not while he was in his doctor mode.

Something had gone wrong. Drastically wrong.

The feel of her face between his hands, the fragrance of her hair, the response that had flared in his gut as their gazes held—all lingered in his mind, taunting him.

When he remembered the slow path her hand had taken down the curve of her hip and along her thigh, desire coursed through him again, startling him with its heat.

She hadn't meant to be provocative—he knew at least that much about her. He'd had more than enough experience, especially since returning to Sugar Falls, with women intent on provocation. A couple of times, he'd entered the examination room to find one of his attractive neighbors striking some sultry pose on the examination table, a sensuous perfume wafting around her like a warning flag.

Pulled muscles seemed to be the ailment of choice among the hometown women lately. That thought brought a rueful twitch to his lips. Gladys had been useful in defusing potentially seductive scenarios. He'd never once become aroused.

Until today. Until he'd gazed into Sarah Flowers's eyes and had wanted more than anything in the world to touch her.

No, he wouldn't have continued with the exam. She needed medical attention, though. She seemed to be suffering from exhaustion, and might have re-injured the wounds she'd mentioned. He also felt certain that she was stressed-out. He wondered why.

Then there was the request Gladys had recorded on her chart: "Wants to know if doctor can determine whether she's had a baby." Sarah had claimed she'd been asking in a general way. Why, then, had she told Gladys that she wanted to know everything he could tell her about herself?

When he'd asked if she'd given birth, she hadn't answered. Could she possibly *not know*? If so, it would mean a serious loss of memory. But she'd denied experiencing any memory loss from the head trauma.

Ms. Sarah Flowers did indeed present a mystery.

He'd told her to leave a number where he could call her with results of tests Gladys had administered. He'd also told her he wanted to see her in a week to follow up on her dizzy spells.

The number she'd left wasn't a valid one, and she hadn't set a follow-up appointment. She also hadn't left an address other than a post-office box, where they'd have to mail the results of the tests. At least it was a local post-office box, he mused, staring down at the chart he'd dropped onto his desk. Which meant she lived here in town.

Which meant he'd see her again, in one way or another.

He smirked and shook his head at himself, bemused by the anticipation that thought provoked. He'd apparently been without a woman for too long. He hadn't dated since he'd been home, which was almost three months now.

Why hadn't he? Part of the reason he'd come back to Sugar Falls was to find someone—a good, honest, uncomplicated woman. *Uncomplicated* was the key word. He'd had all he could take of the other kind. The convoluted relationships he'd found in Boston had taught him a lesson or two…and left him with an empty, lonely feeling that he couldn't quite shake.

He'd thought that coming home might help. So far, it hadn't.

He had no one to blame but himself for his lack of female company. It was high time he started accepting the invitations cast his way, many from women whose families he'd known for years—women who understood the life he meant to make for himself, who enjoyed the sense of kinship and community in Sugar Falls. Women who had no hidden agendas.

The last thing he needed was sexual involvement with a silver-eyed stranger whose gaze simmered with secrets.

But those secrets intrigued him. *She* intrigued him. And the idea of sexual involvement with her made his blood run hot.

He continued poring over her chart.

"YOU TOLD ME HE'D BE grandfatherly. I took that to mean old, Annie. Old, sweet and wise. Not young, handsome and sexy."

Annie Tompkins shrugged. "I thought Doc Brenkowski would be there. I forgot about Connor Wade sharing a practice with him now. But so what if the doctor is young and sexy? That's no reason to chicken out of an exam you really need."

"I didn't chicken out. I postponed it until the doctor of my choice returns to town."

"You chickened out." Before another word could leave Sarah's mouth, Annie held up a halting hand, squared her freckled jaw and squinted against the May sunshine streaming through her open kitchen windows. "No excuses. You march back into that doctor's office, young lady, and have your injuries examined." In mock sternness, Annie added, "Don't make me use force."

Sarah sat back in her chair, relaxing for the first time since leaving Dr. Wade's office that morning. She couldn't imagine this petite retired schoolteacher using force of any kind other than persuasion. In Annie Tompkins, however, persuasion was a force to be reckoned with—the one that had brought Sarah to this quaint mountain town after the Denver hospital had released her.

Breathing in the heady perfume of crabapple, hawthorn and plum blossoms that scented the breeze blowing through the windows, Sarah thought about how glad she was that she'd come home with Annie. Although she hadn't allowed herself to get acquainted with the people of Sugar Falls, the place itself had helped calm her. She felt relatively safe here in this tiny community tucked away in the Colorado Rockies.

Taking advantage of a few stolen moments before returning to the job she'd held for two long weeks, Sarah enjoyed being back in Annie's house again, sipping a freshly brewed cup of her herbal tea. Her employer's grand mansion, luxurious though it was, didn't seem nearly as welcoming. "I'm fine, Annie. Really."

"Fine!" The sun glowed in a halo around Annie's reddish curls, making her look like an exasperated angel in gray sweats. "Just yesterday you got so dizzy, you nearly fell into a laundry basket, according to Lorna Hampton."

Sarah frowned. Her employer hadn't had any business telling Annie about the dizzy spell. "The nurse put me through tests and gave me vitamins to take. The doctor thinks the dizziness is caused by the altitude change, and maybe exhaustion. I'll drink more water, get some rest and be just fine."

"Exhaustion? Lorna's working you too hard, isn't she?"

"Of course not. I enjoy work. I prefer keeping busy. I just haven't been sleeping well, that's all." Which was the truth. The questions and uncertainty about her past kept her awake long into the night, every night...and when sleep finally came, the nightmares woke her.

"You're too stressed-out, and it's all my fault."

"Don't start that again."

"It's true." Annie's thin, freckled face once again reflected the guilt and concern that had ridden so heavily on her throughout the six weeks of their acquaintance. No matter how often Sarah assured her that she didn't blame her for the accident, Annie tormented herself with guilt. "I'm so sorry,

Sarah. If it hadn't been for me, you wouldn't be in this awful predicament. If only I'd been paying closer attention when you stumbled out into that street."

"The accident was my fault, not yours. If your car hadn't hit me, another one would have." Sarah reached for her friend's hands and warmly held them. "You've been an angel, Annie. You took me to the hospital, stayed with me the entire three days, paid all the bills, brought me to your home, nursed me back to health, bought me clothes and helped me find a job."

"Yeah, a job that's driving you to exhaustion." She shook her head sadly. "You're not the house-maid type...and Lorna can't be easy to work for. She's a snob, and her boys are holy terrors. I know she expects you to baby-sit, even though it wasn't part of the job description."

"The job has been fine. I can't tell you how grateful I am to have found it." Jobs, especially ones that included room and board, weren't easy to come by without a work history, references or a social security number.

Annie refused to be pacified. Worry creased her forehead and lined her mouth. "I know you don't like to talk about it, Sarah, but it's been six weeks and you still haven't remembered who you are, where you lived, or anything. I've searched the missing-persons reports over the Internet, I've driven around Denver to police stations and looked at dozens of photos, but I haven't come up with a single clue." She hesitated, and Sarah stiffened, guessing what she'd say next. "I think it's time to go to the authorities or to the media about your amnesia."

"No." A chill of dread went through Sarah. She couldn't tolerate the idea of advertising her weakness to the world and waiting for a stranger to step up and claim her. "I'm not ready to tell anyone yet."

"You're still afraid, aren't you?"

Sarah hesitated, wishing she could evade the question. "Someone was chasing me when I ran out into that street, Annie. I don't remember who or why, but I remember the feeling of utter panic, and knowing that I had to get away. You said it yourself—it looked like I was being chased."

"That's true." Annie regarded her in sympathetic dismay. "Then again, you might have been running for a cab or something. Your fear might be a symptom from the head trauma. After all, it *was* bad enough to cause amnesia."

"I'm sure someone was chasing me. Someone angry, ruthless and violent." She shuddered at the shadow memory that continued to haunt her dreams. Her phantom pursuer might still be hunting for her. "Until I remember more about the situation, I won't go to the authorities or the media. But I do plan to start searching for clues about my past. I'll go back to Denver, to the street where it happened, and see if any memories come back."

"That might work," agreed Annie, although the worry remained on her gently lined face. "But how will you get there? You can't drive, and I won't be here to drive you. Ted insists we leave for our camping trip tomorrow. He's been planning it all year, and I can't talk him out of it."

"Go and have a good time, for heaven's sake. You need the break as much as he does. And please don't worry about me. I'll find a ride when I'm ready to go back to the scene of the accident. And maybe more memories will return on their own." Sarah smiled, determined to be optimistic. "Someone might even issue a bulletin about my disappearance, and I'll learn everything about myself."

Annie nodded and smiled, but Sarah saw the doubt in her eyes. Hurt flickered through her at the thought that this newfound friend might be the only one in the world who cared about her. "I don't want you worrying, Annie."

"Then at least go back to Dr. Wade and tell him about the amnesia. I don't want you passing out somewhere while I'm gone. Your head trauma was serious. You should have a doctor check it."

"I'm sorry, but I can't." Every time she thought about confiding in someone—anyone—a terrible sense of dread stopped her. Word could get around. A story as bizarre as an amnesiac Jane Doe could end up in the newspapers, or even on television. Then who might show up at her door? Her palms began to sweat at the very thought.

She shoved the fear to the back of her mind. She couldn't let it rule her.

But there were practical reasons for keeping the amnesia to herself, too. It wasn't a disorder that most people understood. Annie's husband, the only other person who knew about her memory loss, still didn't trust her. She'd heard him tell Annie, "I don't buy that amnesia story. This isn't some soap opera. I'll keep my mouth shut, if you want, but I'm watching every move she makes."

Sarah could imagine what might happen if the secret of her amnesia got around. Everyone might start suspecting her of some devious motive for coming to town. She could lose her job. Then she'd have to leave the community and start over somewhere new, alone, without knowing anyone at all.

Not even herself.

"At least promise me that if you have another dizzy spell," Annie implored, "you'll go to Dr. Wade about it, even if you don't mention the amnesia. I've known him since he was a teenager. Taught him math in his freshman year. Frankly, I can't remember a more trustworthy, capable student." Annie shook her head at a memory. "That boy was determined to get a scholarship, and by golly, he spent every minute of his high-school years working to make sure he would. He did it, too. Won a scholarship to Harvard. I have to admire him for that, especially considering the family he came from."

"'The family he came from'?"

Annie flushed slightly and hesitated, as if she regretted having broached the subject. "Oh, his parents were always a little...different, that's all. Not that they were *bad* in any way. Their life-style did make things a little harder for Connor, though." After a moment's reflection, she waved her hand in dismissal. "My point is, he overcame all the obstacles and won a scholarship to Harvard. I'm sure he's a wonderful doctor."

"I don't doubt that," Sarah murmured, distracted by the picture Annie had drawn and the questions she had raised. Sarah nearly had to bite her tongue to stop from asking questions about

him. Why should she want to know anything
more? As capable as Connor Wade might be, he
presented a very real danger to her.

She'd been too attracted to him for her own
good. She wouldn't be seeing him again. At least,
she hoped she wouldn't.

"Please, Sarah," persisted Annie. "Promise me
that if you need help while I'm gone, you'll turn to
him. For *my* sake."

Sarah stared in dismay at her friend, her rescuer,
her angel of mercy, whose gaze held a serious plea.
How could she possibly refuse?

She'd just have to make sure that she wouldn't
need help of any kind while Annie was gone. And
she'd have to stop thinking about Dr. Connor
Wade.

2

SHE WAS BACK AGAIN, in his examination room, sitting on the table, with another of those thin paper gowns covering her nakedness. She'd been chilly at first, but as she heard his footsteps approach the room, her tension mounted and her skin grew warm and sensitive.

She'd do it this time. She'd let his large, sundarkened hands slip beneath her paper gown. She'd press herself against those hands, move beneath them, guide them to where she most wanted his touch...and then she'd draw him down in a kiss until he lost all perspective and took her, right there on the table....

Oh, Sarah, really!

Sucking in a large, cooling draught of air, she set her dust cloth and furniture polish aside to press her palms against her heated face. Why couldn't she stop daydreaming about him?

Her fantasies had grown wicked over the course of the week. They'd begun innocently enough. She'd thought about the gazes they'd shared and imagined a deeper meaning to them. She'd added a few intimate whispers, then a stirringly private conversation...and had somehow progressed to this! Good heavens, she'd only met the man once, yet couldn't get him off her mind...or out of her wildest fantasies.

As she forced her attention back to dusting the furniture in the family room, an incredulous question carried on the breeze from the adjoining sundeck where Mimsey Whittenhurst, the willowy blonde from the doctor's office, lounged in the hot tub with Lorna Hampton. "Are you telling me that he asked you out *on a date?*"

Sarah couldn't resist a peek through the open window. Mimsey looked flabbergasted. Sarah moved away from the window and resumed her dusting. Mimsey hadn't seemed to recognize her as the patient who had practically run from Dr. Wade's examining room last week, thank goodness. Perhaps she hadn't even noticed her flight past the nurse's station.

"He's taking me to the Spring Charity Dance at the club tomorrow night," came Lorna's reply. Without even seeing her face, Sarah could picture the young widow's smug smile. She must have bagged some hot date.

Absently Sarah wondered who. Not that she actually cared; she had very little real interest in Lorna's private life, and probably wouldn't know the man, anyway. She'd deliberately avoided people since she'd come to Sugar Falls. Any personal relationship might compromise her secret. Until she remembered more, she'd keep strictly to herself.

That resolve, wise though it was, filled her with an undeniable loneliness. Maybe that was why she'd been so affected by her visit with Dr. Wade. She'd been virtually alone since the accident, with only guilt-ridden Annie to talk to...and now, Annie was gone on her camping trip. Loneliness could be a powerful aphrodisiac, she supposed. Especially when confronted with a man as potently male as Dr. Wade.

"That's just too, *too* fantastic!" Mimsey gushed. Sarah thought she detected a note of envy in her enthusiasm. "I haven't heard of him dating anyone since he came home."

"Me neither." Lorna's reply fairly oozed with self-satisfaction. "Not only that—" she paused, probably to sip her wine cooler and draw out the suspense of the moment "—he's coming to my dinner party tonight."

"You can't mean it! Patsy Jennings is going to be green. Pea green."

"She should have held on to him back in high school. Of course, she's let herself go since then, poor dear."

"She foams at the mouth every time she sees him."

"Don't we all?" The ladies shared a chummy laugh.

Curious now as to who this local heartthrob might be, Sarah waited for another clue as she finished polishing an end table. She supposed she'd find out soon enough. Lorna insisted she help out at the party tonight, along with a waiter from the country club. Sarah planned to work mostly in the kitchen. She didn't want to risk drawing attention to herself. In a town as small as Sugar Falls, questions could be provoked too easily. She couldn't afford questions.

A shriek from the sundeck startled her into

dropping the dust cloth. "My sandals! My new sandals!" Lorna cried. "Tofu, you bad dog. Look what you've done!"

Sarah winced and peered out through the open French doors. Sure enough, Lorna's black-and-white Shih Tzu reclined beside the hot tub with a shredded sandal between his paws. Sarah wished she could somehow spare the dog the punishment that was sure to follow. He was already under too much duress. Lorna's preferential treatment of her new poodle, Fluff-Fluff, was interfering with Tofu's need to stake his claim as the dominant male. Why couldn't Lorna see that? It was perfectly plain to Sarah....

"Sarah!"

She jumped at Lorna's plaintive call, set her bottle of furniture polish aside and hurried out onto the sunny deck where the auburn-haired widow and her elegant blond guest sat in a tiled hot tub, their gold necklaces, earrings and bracelets glittering against well-cultivated tans, their manicured fingers wrapped around tall wine coolers.

Before Sarah could utter a word, Lorna nodded toward the dog whose ears lay back. "Look what he's done to my new sandals. They're a pile of shredded leather. Clean up the mess, please, Sarah, and put Tofu in the broom closet. He's got to learn that spitefulness will get him nowhere." To Mimsey, she confided, "He's been so jealous since I brought Fluff-Fluff home that he's destroyed shoes, clothing, furniture—"

"Since you've mentioned it, Mrs. Hampton," interjected Sarah, pushed beyond her usual prudence by a need to make her understand, "it's really not jealousy causing the problem. It's a dominance issue. Punishing Tofu won't help. You see, he's—"

"Now, Sarah," cooed Lorna in a honeyed tone, "I've asked you to call me 'Miss Lorna.' You're part of the family now."

Frustrated by the interruption, Sarah forced a slight smile. Which other member of the family, she wondered, called her "Miss Lorna"? "Miss Lorna, then. As I was saying, Tofu's resentment probably stems from—"

"And I *know* you're not going to argue with me about how to reprimand my own dog." Beneath Lorna's gracious smile glinted a flash of steel.

"I don't mean to argue, but—"

"Good. Be sure to get all the scraps of leather up off the floor and lock Tofu in the broom closet. And if you haven't finished polishing the silver for tonight, I suggest you concentrate on that for the next few hours." Lorna leaned back against the ledge of the hot tub, closed her eyes and lifted her flawless face to the sun. "The boys have a ball game after school today. Get their uniforms ready, and then walk them down to the park. They have to be there on time. After the game, fix them supper and make sure they bathe."

Biting her tongue to stifle an impulsive reply, Sarah scooped the little black-and-white Shih Tzu up into her arms. If only she didn't need this job so badly, she'd tell Lorna a thing or two about relating to dogs, kids and employees. She did, however, need the job badly.

Persevering against a sudden, dizzying wave of fatigue that she suspected was as much mental as it was physical, she carried the squirming, whining Shih Tzu into the house. She heard Lorna tell Mimsey, "She doesn't have a driver's license. Can you believe it? She has to walk everywhere. It gets annoying."

Sarah almost snorted on her trek through the family room. Lorna thought it was annoying for *her*? Sarah found it almost intolerable that she couldn't simply slide behind the wheel of a car and drive wherever she wanted to go. But how could she apply for a license without identification?

From the open window, she heard Mimsey commiserate with Lorna. "It's *s-o-o-o* hard to find good help, isn't it?"

Sarah rolled her eyes on her way to the kitchen. She hoped they'd both get wrinkles from too much sun.

Mildly ashamed of herself for such a thought, she installed Tofu in the broom closet and surreptitiously supplied him with toys and other comfort items. She then raised her chin with determined pride and returned to the sundeck to clean up the mess of shredded leather. As she drew close, she was relieved to hear that the women had finished their disparaging appraisal of her and had apparently returned to their original topic of conversation.

"You don't mind my dating him, do you?" Lorna was asking Mimsey.

"Mind! Why should *I* mind?"

"Oh, c'mon, Mims. Why else would you have taken a job?" Lorna let out a sly little chuckle. "I can't blame you for wanting to, er, get to know him better."

After an initial huff and bluster of protest, Mimsey gave in to a sheepish giggle. "Well, I suppose that *is* one of the most alluring benefits of the job...getting chummy with the boss."

Sarah froze just inside the open doorway of the family room. *They were talking about Dr. Wade.* They had to be. Mimsey worked in his office...and he was definitely a heartthrob. Which meant he'd asked Lorna Hampton out on a date. A curious lump of misery formed in Sarah's stomach.

The earlier part of their conversation replayed in her mind, and another startling realization hit her. *He'd be coming to the dinner party tonight.*

THE MOUNTAINS THEMSELVES were decked out in full spring dress for the party, bright with pink, yellow and indigo wildflowers lacing their verdant slopes—a vivid backdrop for the rolling green golf course that adjoined Lorna's backyard.

A peal of thunder and a flash of lightning, however, announced a quick change of plans for an outdoor supper on the brick patio. Dodging huge, cold raindrops, Sarah and a waiter from Sugar Falls Country Club moved the elegant table settings into the dining room, while Lorna welcomed her guests into the spacious formal living room at the front of the mansion.

Sarah hoped to stay out of sight for the entire evening and work behind the scenes in the kitchen. André, the slim, balding waiter with an engaging smile and European charm, had plenty of experience serving at parties. Surely he could handle this private dinner for ten.

Through the French doors that led from the dining room to the living room, Sarah caught a glimpse of the guests, dressed in casual yet elegant attire, laughing and chatting around trays of hors d'oeuvres set on various tables. Most of the guests, Sarah had learned from André, were members of the country club or patrons of the nearby ski resort that Lorna owned.

Sarah wondered if Dr. Connor Wade had arrived yet.

He's not going to notice you, she assured herself. *You're just the hired help.* And if he did, so what? Regardless of how insulted he might have felt about her demanding another doctor, he surely wouldn't mention her visit in a social situation, would he? Of course not. He probably wouldn't acknowledge her presence at all. Servants were virtually invisible at functions like these.

Still, she breathed a sigh of relief when she'd finished setting the long, linen-covered table in the dining room and retreated to the sanctuary of the kitchen, where she arranged appetizers on trays.

It actually wasn't Dr. Wade's reaction that concerned her, she realized. It was her own. She'd been so powerfully attracted to him that she'd nearly made a fool of herself in his office last week. She'd sat in dumbstruck silence for most of her visit, then blurted out that ridiculous comment about the calluses on his hands. If she couldn't trust her own decorum in his presence, she had to maintain a safe distance. A buffer zone.

"Will you pour four glasses of Chardonnay, please, *chérie?*" André asked. "I'll be back for them."

She nodded, admiring the waiter's upbeat energy. She needed some of that energy. Her own was seriously flagging. The day had been a long one...and rife with the oddest mix of anxiety and anticipation.

She didn't want to see Dr. Connor Wade again. Yet, her pulse beat faster at the very thought.

Forcing him out of her mind, she poured wine into delicate crystal flutes. Light shimmered through the pale, fragrant Chardonnay, and suddenly a memory materialized. *She'd been holding a crystal flute like this one, lifting a cool, fragrant glass of wine in some toast.*

A memory! An honest-to-goodness memory! She set down the wineglass to stop from spilling it as excitement fizzled through her. She'd been so afraid that memories would never return...and now this one had. Closing her eyes, she savored the brief, remembered scene, then tried to recall more, to see the people she'd been with or identify the place.

No other details surfaced.

Though somewhat disappointed, she finished pouring the wine with a much lighter heart. At least a fragment of memory had returned. And although she couldn't be sure, she believed the toast had been made in her honor. A celebration of some kind. What had she been celebrating?

Distracted by her speculation, she was taken completely off guard by the sound of a low, masculine voice that reached her ears from the living room. She recognized the voice...and her own warm, sensual reaction to it.

He was here.

She fervently renewed her resolve to spend the

evening in the kitchen and found plenty to keep her busy. Her luck held all the way through the predinner cocktails, soup, salad and the main course.

The problem came with dessert. "While I'm serving the pie and ice cream," André instructed, "you pour the coffee." No argument would sway him. The ice cream would melt before the coffee was served if Sarah didn't pour.

She considered feigning an illness, but couldn't stand to ruin André's presentation. He took such pride in his work.

You're bound to run into Dr. Wade sooner or later...especially if he's dating Lorna.

With that grim thought, she took the coffeepot in hand and followed André. As she neared the ornately carved archway of the dining-room entrance, she heard the cheerful hum of conversation; saw the warm glow of the crystal chandelier reflected in the polished paneling; picked out the deep, almost musical voice of Dr. Wade relaying some lighthearted anecdote.

She saw him the moment she rounded the corner. He lounged in his chair at the center of the long table and spoke with a casual, humorous charm that kept everyone attentive and smiling. Dressed in a silky dark shirt left open at his strong throat and a charcoal-gray jacket that snugly fit his powerful shoulders, he looked elegant in a virile, nonchalant way that tugged at something feminine and primitive within her. If she'd thought him handsome the other day in his lab coat and jeans, he was nothing short of devastating now.

Lorna Hampton sat on his right side, looking

slim and tan in a peach satin blouse and pearls that perfectly complemented her auburn prettiness. Mimsey, with an elaborate coiffure, sat on his left in a low-cut beige-lace top.

Highly conscious of her own drab white blouse, black skirt and red apron, her hair escaping the twist she'd hurriedly pinned at the top of her head, Sarah felt like a scrubwoman after a long day's work.

As a matter of fact, she *was* a scrubwoman after a long day's work.

And, by golly, she refused to feel socially inferior because of it! She was earning an honest wage. She had nothing to feel ashamed of. Squaring her shoulders, she paused at the nearest guest's chair, lifted the coffee cup and poured the steaming, redolent brew with as much grace as she could command.

"The dean had an Arabian stallion in his stable," Dr. Wade was saying, a note of amused recollection in his tone, "one of the finest I've ever seen— jet-black, muscular and high-spirited, with a full, flowing mane and tail—as wild as he was pretty."

Sarah moved to the next guest, who was seated across the table from the man she refused to look at. So, he liked horses. Loved them, from the sound of it. Why should that move her? Why should that tempt her to set aside her coffeepot and lose herself in his tale?

Lifting another cup, she poured.

His soft, reminiscent chuckle punctuated the story. "The dean's daughter, who, at the all-knowing age of eighteen, considered herself the world's best horsewoman, tried to saddle him. You should have seen when she—"

He broke off suddenly, mid-sentence.

Trying not to wonder what had interrupted his conversational flow and thrown the room into silence, Sarah concentrated on her pouring.

"The dean's daughter tried to saddle him, and…?" prompted Lorna, sounding somewhat bemused.

But he didn't pick up on his cue. Sarah couldn't resist a quick peek at his face.

A mistake.

Her gaze connected solidly with his. He was staring at her with such a look of surprise that self-conscious heat climbed up her neck and into her face. Oh, he recognized her, all right. No doubt about that. She quickly wrenched her gaze away from his, just in time to realize that she'd picked up a sugar bowl instead of a coffee cup. Embarrassed, she set it back down and reached for the cup beside it.

The doctor's silence stretched on as the guests waited for the end of his story. From her peripheral vision, she realized that he continued to stare. The others had begun to slant curious gazes her way. And why wouldn't they? He was gaping at her in the rudest manner possible.

"You were saying, Connor?" Lorna's prompting now sounded rather peevish. She obviously wasn't pleased at having her trophy date's attention snared by the hired help.

"Uh, yes…" he said, sounding as if he hadn't a clue as to what he'd been saying.

"The girl tried to saddle the stallion, and...?" Lorna repeated.

"She did a damn fine job of it, too," he murmured. No one could doubt that his mind wasn't on his words.

Although she didn't chance another look at him, Sarah knew he watched her as she made her way to the end of the table. She'd be starting down the other side soon, heading his way. She wasn't sure she could take his scrutiny at close range....

"Actually, the problem came in when she mounted the horse," he finally went on, relaxing in his chair and warming to his story again. Sarah felt immeasurably relieved that the spotlight of his attention had, apparently, shifted elsewhere. "She ended up on her backside," he said. "And when I tried to help her up, she did the oddest thing. She snatched her hand away from mine. Said she didn't like the feel of the, uh, *calluses* on my hand."

Sarah's breath caught in her throat, and she sloshed coffee over the rim of a cup she was holding, burning her fingers.

"What do you think, ladies?" Though he addressed the table at large, he was watching Sarah, with his head cocked and a teasing gleam in his hazel eyes. "Are calluses on a man's hands *that* disturbing?"

The women replied all at once, their comments, retorts and giggles blending into one mocking roar in Sarah's ears. Though the others didn't realize it, he was making fun of her! Would a pot of hot coffee in his lap, she wondered, be "*that* disturbing"?

André, thank goodness, had finished serving the pie. Without a word of explanation, Sarah handed the coffeepot to him and strode out of the dining room.

Never had she been so humiliated.

At least, not that she could recall.

CONNOR SAT STARING in the direction Sarah Flowers had taken, barely acknowledging the response his nonsensical question had garnered from the women at the table.

He'd almost given up on finding her. He'd watched for her everywhere, expecting to see her in town, or to hear about a newcomer who matched her description. But no one mentioned her at all. At least, not within his hearing.

He'd stopped short of asking around. He hadn't wanted to draw attention to his interest in her—not until he knew who she was and why she was here. Maybe not even then. She wasn't the kind of woman he'd moved home to find. She was a stranger, a mystery, a complication waiting to happen...the last thing in the world he wanted.

He'd done his level best to forget her.

It hadn't worked.

Tonight, for the first time since she'd bolted from his examination room, he'd managed to stop thinking about her, thanks to the distraction of Lorna's party. Then, in the middle of telling some silly story, he'd glanced up and she was there.

The surprise of it knocked the words right out of him. She looked pale, and fragile, and so damn pretty with her hair escaping its heavy upsweep and curling in wisps around her face that he simply couldn't help staring. What was she doing here?

Serving coffee, obviously.

Before he had time to think much about that, she'd lifted her incredibly sensual gaze to him, and thinking became impossible. Her face warmed to the color he remembered from their first meeting, when he'd touched her. A powerful longing welled up in him to touch her again—at his leisure this time, in ways that would make her tremble and groan. Wicked, wonderful ways that would set them both on fire...

It unnerved him, this crazy desire provoked by the mere sight of her. He was stronger than that—a man of principle, and logic, and reason; not a slave to carnal impulse. He would ignore the heat she ignited down low in his body. Ignore the musings of what she'd look like, what she'd feel like, in his bed.

But then she turned away without the slightest acknowledgement, as if she'd never seen him before, and all thought of resisting her evaporated. She meant to ignore him, did she? Pretend they'd never met? Not if he could help it...

He had to grit his teeth and reminded himself that she had every right to pretend they'd never met. As a patient, she was guaranteed absolute confidentiality.

Yet, on a purely personal level, he couldn't tolerate her ignoring him. He wanted to tease her into a response. Even the slightest response—a smile, or a frown, or an acknowledging gaze—would do. She owed him that much, for all the sleepless nights she'd caused him.

With a cleverness he felt rather proud of, he interjected her complaint about his callused hands into the story he'd been telling.

She didn't give herself away by much—not enough for anyone else to notice. But her spine stiffened; her voluptuous mouth tightened; and for a moment, he thought she meant to dump the pot of coffee in his lap.

The interaction with her, low-key though it was, brought him strangely alive. He was ready to dodge whatever she might throw at him, grab her, whisk her outside...punish her with long, thorough kisses....

Yes, indeed, he was ready.

Instead, she turned and stalked from the room.

Where had she gone? Was she leaving? What had she been doing here, anyway? Did she work for Lorna, or maybe for the country club, as André did? Was it a onetime gig?

Would he see her again?

Tossing his napkin aside, he pushed himself away from the table. Something had to be settled between them, one way or another.

"Excuse me," he murmured to Lorna and the others who seemed to be watching. "I have some business to take care of." Before anyone could ask for details, he headed in the direction his mystery woman had taken.

He wouldn't let her get away from him so easily this time.

3

SHE WASN'T IN THE KITCHEN, or down the connecting hallway, or in the utility room near the back door. Just when he reached the conclusion that she'd left the premises altogether, he caught sight of movement through a window.

She was out there, in the backyard.

His heart turned over. He had another chance. He pushed through the door onto the deck and descended the steps to the brick walkway that led through the blossoming, rain-scented garden. The rain had ceased, but a light mist clung to his face as he walked.

She'd stopped on the small decorative bridge that crossed a rushing mountain stream. Leaning against the white rail, she stared out into the mist. His footsteps alerted her, and she turned with a start.

Her look of dismay stopped him on the brick walkway. They stared at each other in tense silence. Her midnight hair was damp and curling in loose tendrils around her pale, oval face…a face he'd seen often in his daydreams lately.

"What are you doing out here?" she finally asked, her eyes wide and wary, the same silver gray as the mist surrounding them.

He thrust his hands into his trouser pockets and

assumed a relaxed stance. He couldn't remember the last time a woman had failed to welcome him anywhere, unless he counted his last meeting with her. "Funny, but I was going to ask you the same."

"That's none of your business, Dr. Wade."

"Connor," he said. "My name's Connor."

She looked away from him, out over the brook, her profile lush and beguiling. She was doing it again, he noticed. Ignoring him. He had no idea how to break through the barrier she was erecting, or why she felt she needed it.

"Do you work for Lorna?" he asked, doubting that she did. Maybe she'd volunteered for some reason to help out at the party.

"Yes, I do."

That surprised him. He didn't particularly like the idea of her working for Lorna, nor did he understand it. Something didn't fit. "As...?"

"A maid."

He had a hard time seeing her in that role. Her refined manner of speaking and regal bearing gave him the impression that she'd been highly educated and raised to mingle at the most exclusive society functions. What had led her to take this job as Lorna's maid?

More questions, he realized. Every moment he spent with this woman only piled new questions on top of old ones. He intended to have answers to every one of them before he was through with her. "You didn't make an appointment for a follow-up visit. Are you taking my other advice—bed rest, vitamins, no heavy lifting?"

She rounded on him, her face alive with indignation. "I won't make another appointment with you, and I won't answer to you about my health. I thought I'd made myself clear. I don't want you as my doctor."

He strolled closer and gazed more directly into her eyes. "And I don't want you as my patient."

Surprise glittered in those rain-gray depths—surprise, and maybe a little affront. Unable to stop his gaze from wandering, he noticed mist beaded on her skin. And her lips, like a pale pink rosebud, glistened with dewy moisture.

"Then what do you want?" she breathed.

You. He didn't say it, but he felt it, and from the way her face warmed with color, he sensed that she read him perfectly. She backed away from him slightly; a telling movement.

He rested his forearms on the railing beside her. "You always seem to be running away from me. Why?"

She let out a soft, exasperated breath. "What does it matter? You don't know me, and I don't know you. That's not about to change. You should go back in to the party. They'll be looking for you."

"Tell me."

Her lips compressed and she looked away. He continued to study her, thoroughly intrigued by the emotion she fought to suppress. At least she felt *something* toward him.

After a few silent moments, his patience paid off. Her mouth quirked in surrender, and she confronted him, full face. "If you must know, you embarrassed me in there."

He frowned, baffled. Although he *had* deliberately teased her about the calluses, he didn't see how she could be embarrassed by a joke that only she and he would understand. "How did I embarrass you?"

"You mean you don't know?"

"No."

"You stopped in the middle of your horse story and...and gaped at me."

"'Gaped'?" He thought back to when he'd first seen her tonight, unsure of how he had acted. He'd been aware only of her. "I gaped?"

"Yes, you gaped. Which made everyone else gape at me, too. And then you had to bring up—" she hesitated, looking discomfited "—your calluses."

"So?"

"So! You did it deliberately," she accused. "You know you did."

"But not to embarrass you. I don't see how it could. After all, no one else there knows how you feel about my hands."

Her lips parted in protest. "I don't feel *anything* about your hands!" In her pique, she had lost a good deal of her stiffness and her eyes sparkled with lively annoyance.

He couldn't have been more enchanted. "Then why did you complain about them in my office?"

"I wasn't complaining about them." Her embarrassment flared visibly. "I just...noticed them, that's all. Their hardness, I mean." She bit down on her shapely lower lip, and her hands gripped the railing. After a moment, she admitted in a soft, pained voice, "I had no business noticing something like that. Something so...personal. I'm sorry."

"It didn't bother me." Other things about her

bothered him, though. Like the apple-blossom scent of her hair, the luminescent quality of her skin, the inviting smoothness of her mouth and the way her damp cotton blouse clung to her, almost transparent in places. Private, intriguing places that he longed to explore. To feel. To taste...

He struggled to speak past the heat rising in him. "So my hands aren't the reason you don't want me as your doctor?"

"Of course not," she scoffed.

"Then what is?"

A stillness settled between them, and he swore he could hear her heart pounding in double time. Or maybe it was his heart, or both of theirs, beating in unison.

She turned a solemn gaze to him. "Why don't *you*," she whispered, "want *me* as your patient?"

"Because," he replied with a huskiness he couldn't help, "I want you in another capacity altogether."

The admission electrified something between them; something as elusive as the garden-scented mist, but no less real.

The guarded look returned to her face. "Then the problem should be easy to understand. I'm only in the market for a doctor. If you'll excuse me, I have work to do." She made a move to pass by him.

He realized he'd made a grave tactical error. He'd given her a concrete reason to avoid him. "Sarah." He blocked her way, impulsively catching her by the shoulders to hold her fast, to keep her from escaping him again. "I wasn't trying to come on to you. I was just being honest. Can't we have *that* between us, at least—simple honesty?"

She didn't pull away from him, as he half expected, or order him to let her go. She went perfectly still, then lifted her face to his, as if arrested by what he'd said.

"Honesty?" A rueful smile softened her mouth. "Thank you for your honesty, Connor." The sound of his name in her low, feminine voice pleased him, but he barely had time to savor it. His attention was riveted by the surprising gentleness in her gaze—a warm, womanly gentleness that magnified her beauty tenfold. "I'm flattered to know that I'm not the only one feeling this…this chemistry between us."

Before he could find his voice to reply, her eyes had darkened, her gaze dipped to his mouth, and her gentleness took on a sensual hue, making his body harden and his blood rush. Her fingertips grazed his face—a brief, tender caress that he felt to his very core. "But I can't get involved with you. So please," she implored, "stay away from me."

Before her words registered clearly, she eased out of his grasp and hurried down the walkway.

He stared after her, mesmerized by the promise of heaven he'd found in her eyes, her voice, her body…and stunned by the blow of her words. *Stay away from me.*

He shook his head to cast off the dazed feeling and struggled to make sense of what she'd said. Had she really gazed at him with such honeyed softness, touched him with such tender warmth, stirred him with such blazing sensuality…and told him to stay away?

Did she really think he would?

If so, he'd have to add one more symptom to her medical chart. *Delusional.*

BY THE TIME SHE REACHED the house, the mist had turned into a cold drizzle, and her sensual reaction to Connor Wade had turned into an uncontrollable trembling. She wished she could forget about the party in progress and rush to the privacy of her small attic bedroom.

But as she rounded the corner to the kitchen, she nearly plowed into Lorna, who seemed to be waiting for her like a spider in a web, ready to pounce.

"There you are. I've been looking all over for you." Lorna inspected her with barely disguised disapproval. "You're wet. Where have you been?"

"Outside. I needed a break."

"A break? I see. I should have known a rainstorm wouldn't interfere with *that.*" Her mouth thinned, but after a moment, relaxed again, and her voice lost its cutting edge, although Sarah clearly sensed her tension. "Did you happen to see one of my guests? The gentleman who was sitting next to me at the table?"

"No, I didn't." She couldn't afford to alienate Lorna with the truth, and hoped she'd never learn of the white lie.

Lorna seemed somewhat mollified, but not entirely. "You do know who I'm talking about, don't you? Dr. Connor Wade."

"I believe so."

"Then…you do know him?"

"By sight, I suppose."

Lorna allowed herself a small, tight smile. "He must have gone to some private corner to take a call. A definite downside to dating a doctor—they always seem to be on duty."

Sarah took that to be notification of the fact that Lorna was dating him. She apparently had noticed the attention Connor had paid her at the table. Good thing Lorna hadn't heard or seen him in the garden, whispering that he wanted her...holding her with his hard, warm, controlling hands... gazing at her as if he intended to kiss her senseless.

Warmth tingled through her at the memory. At least she knew now that the intoxicating attraction she felt for him wasn't entirely one-sided. Still, she couldn't allow herself to be swept away by physical longing. She couldn't afford to form attachments of any kind.

Even if she could, she'd keep her distance from him. For all she knew, he might make a practice of flattering and seducing vulnerable women while dating wealthy socialites like Lorna. For some reason, it hurt too much to entertain that possibility.

"André was concerned when he couldn't find you," continued Lorna. "He's serving the after-dinner cordials now, and then he'll be leaving. He doesn't do dishes. It's not in *his* job description." Her slight emphasis on the word "his" reminded Sarah that dishwashing was certainly in her job description.

Gripping the edge of the marble kitchen counter, Sarah fought off the gray, smothering fatigue that pressed in on her. She'd started work so early that morning, and had barely taken a break or eaten a bite. Not that she was hungry. Her stomach felt too knotted, her eyes too heavy, her head too light. She truly felt as if she might pass out.

If only she could sleep at night, the days wouldn't be taking such a toll. But the questions and the nightmares refused to let her rest. She was caught between long days and sleepless nights. Maybe tonight would be different. Maybe tonight she'd sleep.

"Would you mind if I do them tomorrow?" she managed to ask. "I'll have them done first thing, bright and early."

"You mean, you want to leave all these dirty dishes in my kitchen overnight?"

Sarah's heart sank. Lorna obviously meant to have no mercy. She wouldn't lower her pride by asking again. She wouldn't give the woman the satisfaction. She'd rather wash every damn dish in the house, if it took her all night.

She swayed on her feet.

"I'll pay André extra to do them." The deep, brusque voice from the kitchen doorway drew both women's attention. "Or I'll do them myself."

"Connor!" Lorna's face had flushed, her voice had risen in pitch, and her hand fluttered to her hair to smooth it. "Don't be silly. Why in the world should you—" Her exclamation broke off as she stared at him.

He leaned against the doorjamb in his water-stained sport coat, his hands in the pockets of his damp trousers, his short hair darker and spikier than usual, glistening with moisture.

Lorna's gaze slowly returned to Sarah, whose clothes were also damp, whose hair also sparkled with rain. No one could doubt that they'd both been outside. Most likely, together.

Sarah stood clinging to the kitchen counter in mute dismay.

"It doesn't take a medical genius to realize that she's on the verge of a collapse," Connor remarked, his gaze connecting with Sarah's. "I suggest she take it easy for the next couple days and get some bed rest—along with plenty of fluids and vitamins. She's obviously not far from physical exhaustion."

"Physical exhaustion," Lorna repeated. "I had no idea." With only a stiff lip indicating her dismay, she schooled her features into a semblance of courteous interest. "Is she a patient of yours, Connor?"

"No!" Sarah finally managed to exclaim. "I am *not* a patient of his." She realized then that she'd blown the only excuse that might have explained why they'd been speaking together in private. "I mean, I'm not *technically* a patient of his. I went to see Dr. Brenkowski, who happened to be out of the country—" she hadn't meant to tell Lorna any of this! "—but there's absolutely nothing wrong with me."

"Maybe not, but until Doc Brenkowski gets back, I'm in charge of all the patients, and what I say goes." A wry gleam entered his hazel eyes. "Medically speaking, that is."

Sarah drew in an angry breath. "You are not, and never will be, my doctor."

"Sarah," Lorna admonished. "Really! Let's not forget our manners. He is, after all, my guest."

Ignoring Lorna's interjection and pacing a few

steps closer to Sarah, Connor warned, "Ignore my advice, sweetheart, and you'll end up in one of the beds in my clinic."

"Oh, my," Lorna murmured. "We don't want that."

"My name's not 'sweetheart.'" She realized she was grasping at straws now, but didn't care. Maybe the word wouldn't have bothered her as much if he hadn't succeeded in making it sound like an endearment. She couldn't take any form of endearment from him right now. She was simply too worn down and angry and vulnerable to keep it in perspective.

"Go to bed, Sarah," he commanded, "and stay there."

"By all means, go to bed," Lorna concurred. "I insist." Her jade-green eyes now glittered with what could pass for concern. "Either André or I will do the dishes. You concentrate on taking care of yourself, hmm?"

Sensing that she couldn't win this fight—and not even sure what would constitute a win—Sarah lifted her chin and headed for her bedroom. Through her resentment and mind-numbing fatigue, she heard Connor call André aside and mutter something to him.

"Put your money away, Connor," Lorna said. "I'll pay him."

"Let me. Consider it my way of freeing up the rest of your evening." Connor's voice held a smile—a lazy, sexy smile, Sarah guessed. "You and I have barely had time to talk."

Hurrying out of earshot, Sarah gripped the handrail with a vengeance as she started on the second flight of stairs to her attic bedroom. He would spend the evening with her employer. Would he gaze at her the same way he'd gazed at her, and whisper the same kind of heart-stopping nonsense?

The idea bothered her far more than it should have.

There was only one thing she knew for certain about Dr. Connor Wade: The man posed a definite danger to her—emotionally, socially and financially.

With a few indiscreet words, he could have the town buzzing with suspicious questions about her. The prospect of anyone prying into her business renewed the fear she'd been trying to tame.

And he definitely endangered her job—a job she desperately needed. With no home, car, references, social security number or savings, she'd be in terrible straits without it. Especially with Annie gone for the next few weeks.

Regardless of how much pride she'd have to swallow, she'd make it her top priority to win back Lorna's trust...and to avoid Dr. Dark 'n' Handsome as if her life depended on it.

In a way, she supposed it did.

WITH HIS FACE SHADED FROM the noonday sun by his old brown Stetson, Connor guided his horse down the last of the steep, rocky slopes, then urged her into a canter across a grassy field.

The unusually warm weather for May had brought out a profusion of wildflowers, lush greenery and wildly singing birds. He savored the heady scent of mountain flora, the song of the warblers and the dense, summer-like heat, glad that he'd finished his Saturday-morning rounds early.

Most of the families he'd visited farther up in the mountains had been out, away from their isolated, rough-hewn cabins, probably frolicking at waterfalls and swimming holes. Only the oldest and sickest had been on hand.

As he drew closer to home, Connor wondered if his nurse Gladys had returned from the visit she'd agreed to make for him. He'd promised to bring her a loaf of homemade bread if she'd drop by Lorna's and casually check up on Sarah Flowers—just to make sure she was okay. Knowing Gladys, she might also engage Sarah in a little fact-finding chat.

He wouldn't be averse to that.

Lorna hadn't told him much last night. All he'd learned was that Sarah was a cousin of Annie Tompkins, and she planned to stay in Sugar Falls for the summer; through autumn, at the most. From clues Annie had dropped, Lorna guessed that Sarah had just come through a divorce.

Connor hoped Lorna was wrong—for Sarah's sake, he told himself. A woman he'd dated in Boston had been recently divorced and spent too much time dwelling on past betrayals. She'd then allowed her ex to sleep on her couch whenever he came to town. The situation had grown too complicated for Connor, and he'd sworn to stay away from newly divorced women. Not that she'd broken his heart or upset him too greatly. He'd never been fool enough to allow anyone that much power over his state of mind.

He had to admit, though, that his state of mind

had been seriously affected lately. He'd spent another long night wrestling with questions about Sarah Flowers.

She certainly seemed to be hiding something—writing false phone numbers on her medical chart; telling him with her eyes and her touch that she wanted him, but with her words to stay away. "I can't get involved with you."

Why the hell couldn't she?

By morning, he'd come to his senses. Whatever secrets she was hiding, the woman was a living, breathing complication who had already cost him too many sleepless nights. Besides, she planned to leave town in a few months' time.

He had to get over his crazy infatuation with her. Pursuing her could damage more promising relationships—not a smart move for a single man in a small town.

He did, however, feel somewhat concerned about her health. She really had been on the verge of collapse last night.

As he drew closer, he saw Gladys waiting near the stable, leaning up against her old blue Chevy with a disapproving slant to her mouth. She didn't hold with his "tending to folks too ornery to visit the office," as she described his Saturday-morning rounds.

She didn't understand the life-style these avid nature-lovers had chosen, living "off the grid"—without power or running water. Most were aging hippies, artists and musicians who had settled in these Colorado Rockies during the sixties, raising their kids with a reverence for nature, art and rock 'n' roll, along with a disdain for society. Not only would they not visit his office, but they wouldn't have accepted his much-needed help if they hadn't considered him one of their own.

He understood these proud, visionary-artist types. His parents had been among the most visionary.

"What did you bring home today, Medicine Man?" his spry, gray-haired nurse teased, dressed in an oversize University of Colorado shirt and shorts. "Since I don't hear any squawking, I'm assuming no one paid you with live chickens this time."

Connor smiled and tipped his hat back as he brought his horse to a dancing halt. "No live chickens, but a hand-carved flute and brace of fresh trout. And for you—" he dug into his saddlebag and came up with a redolent loaf of brick-oven bread "—I think they called it 'zucchini 'n' sunflower seed.'" He tossed the loaf to Gladys and dismounted. "You did check up on Sarah Flowers for me, didn't you?"

"I dropped by Lorna's, but Sarah wasn't in bed. She was working."

He scowled. He'd warned both her and Lorna that she needed a couple days of bed rest. "Working at what?"

"When I first got there, she was cooking breakfast. Then the two dogs started fighting. When I left, Lorna was threatening to get rid of one of the dogs, the kids were pitching a fit about it, and Sarah was holding the Shih Tzu while trying to coax the poodle out from under the side porch."

Connor was distracted from his annoyance by the picture those words had drawn. Sarah apparently felt comfortable with animals. He'd been hoping to find out she hated them, or hated kids...anything that might tarnish her appeal. He supposed the anti-children sentiment was still possible. Maybe having to deal with Lorna's two rambunctious boys accounted for her stress. It wouldn't be hard to imagine; veteran dads and baseball coaches had a hard time managing the Hampton boys.

"That gal does look pale as a ghost," Gladys went on. "I thought she was going to pass out over the hot stove. She told me she was fine, though, and that you should mind your own business." She paused, and a watchful glint entered her blue eyes. "Good thing she's not our concern."

Connor's fist tightened around the lead shank as he led his horse toward the stable. She really wasn't their concern. Why couldn't he get that through his head?

"She volunteered to take the kids to their golf lesson at the club," Gladys chatted, "then to watch them at the pool."

Anger rose in him—at both Sarah for her stubborn refusal to stay in bed and at Lorna for not insisting on it.

"She'll probably watch the kids tonight, too, while you take Lorna to the dance." Gladys walked to the driver's side of her car with the freshly baked bread cradled to her chest. "Guess I'll get going. Told my grandkids I'd take them to the lake for a swim. How about you, Doc? I'll pack an extra towel. The kids love to gang up on you in the water."

"Sounds like fun," he replied, preoccupied, "but I've got something else in mind for this afternoon."

She paused beside her driver's door. "Oh?"

He glanced away, not really wanting to tell her. When she continued to wait in expectant silence, he muttered, "Thought I'd stop by the club for a round of golf, or a game of tennis."

"Or…a swim in the pool?"

"Now that you mention it—" he met her probing gaze with a wry half smile "—a swim does sound rather refreshing."

4

AFTER MAKING HER WAY through an obstacle course of exuberant kids and sunbathing mothers, Sarah hailed the lounge chair as a blessed refuge—a place where she could lie down, if only for a little while, and watch her two charges swim.

She hoped they'd do so without fighting. During their golf lesson, ten-year-old Jeffrey had "accidentally" swatted his little brother in the rump with a club. Timmy had charged him like a raging bull. They'd poked and tripped each other throughout their practice swings, then raced to the locker room where Timmy hid Jeffrey's swim trunks.

If only she'd gotten a little more sleep last night, Sarah felt sure she could have controlled the boys better. At least here at the pool, a stern-looking female lifeguard with a piercing whistle was helping to keep all the children in line.

Straining to keep her eyes open despite the powerful afternoon sun, Sarah wished she wasn't so tired. She hoped the megadose of caffeine in her soda would kick in soon.

Punch Cola…ten times stronger than coffee, or so the golf pro had told her. He'd noticed her sleepiness during the boys' lesson and tossed her an icy bottle that she hadn't been able to refuse.

She tipped the bottle back and drank the last few swallows. She had to wake herself up.

She hadn't slept much last night. The nightmare had woken her again. She'd sat up in the dark, trembling and sweating from the horror of the chase. A faceless phantom had been tracking her through crowds of strangers, drawing closer with every step.

She hadn't been able to get back to sleep. Timmy and Jeffrey had leaped onto her bed at the first light of dawn, demanding eggs and pancakes. As she'd cooked, Lorna had purred, "Sarah, dear, are you sure you won't exhaust yourself, scrambling all those eggs? Maybe you need an extended vacation."

Her sarcasm had spelled out a clear message: She'd have to work doubly hard to make up for last night. That prospect didn't bother her, but she felt her energy seriously lagging from her many sleepless nights.

The dogs, meanwhile, had started a fight over territorial rights. Sometime in the middle of the ruckus, Dr. Wade's nurse had dropped by for a "casual visit." Lorna had seemed surprised at the visit—Gladys obviously didn't drop by very often—and Gladys had made a point of asking Sarah how she felt.

The idea of Connor Wade sending his nurse to check up on her made Sarah's blood boil. He'd already endangered her job!

She shut her eyes against the bright, hot sun and tried not to think about him, or his evening with Lorna last night, or their date for the dance tonight.

His relationship with Lorna didn't matter to her in the least.

So why had she been dwelling on it all morning?

She heard the scraping of a chair being dragged to a spot close beside her and heard feminine voices calling out greetings like, "What a surprise to see you here," and, "Why aren't you out on the lake fishing, Doc?"

Sarah stiffened. Had they really said "Doc," or was she fixating on her resentment against the infuriating local doctor?

A deep, good-natured rumble of a reply brought her eyes open. Turning her head, she came face-to-face with the man himself. Dr. Connor Wade, in the flesh. Smooth, tightly muscled flesh, at that...with a gleaming tan and rolling biceps.

"Afternoon, Ms. Flowers." He'd settled into a poolside armchair and spread his muscle-corded legs out in front of him. He wore blue swim trunks and sandals—nothing else—which left his broad, well-honed chest bare. Elegant swirls of maple-golden curls encircled masculine nipples, then tapered down to a flat, lean stomach. Sunlight touched off highlights in his tawny hair and vivid hazel eyes.

He met her gaze and smiled.

She shut her eyes and groaned.

"I wanted to apologize for last night." His low, gruff voice was meant only for her. "I know you were upset by my, uh, interference. I meant it for the best."

She didn't want to talk to him. His nearness caused a tightening below her stomach and a warming in her blood. Her beige, one-piece suit—

more modest than most—suddenly felt too revealing, the way it clung to her body and cut away high at her hips. Her prickly awareness of Connor's gaze made her head swim.

"I asked you to stay away from me," she admonished in a tense whisper.

"That's another thing I wanted to tell you. I've thought about what you said, and realize you were right." Hesitating briefly, he glanced at her eyes, then at her mouth. "We can't get involved."

She tried not to show her surprise. After his interference last night and his deployment of Gladys this morning, she hadn't expected such an easy victory.

And she hadn't expected the hurt that lanced through her. What had changed his mind? The evening he'd spent with Lorna?

"So, you see, you don't have to avoid me," he pointed out, "or run away every time you see my face. As you suggested to Gladys this morning, I'll, uh, mind my own business."

Her throat felt curiously tight. "Thank you."

He lapsed into silence and she turned her face away from him, looking for the kids. They were splashing around in the shallow end of the pool. All she had to do was watch them, she told herself. She didn't have to think about how alone she suddenly felt in the world.

"If you'd like, I can move my chair elsewhere," he offered.

"Sit wherever you want, Dr. Wade."

Their sideways gazes locked, and she thought he was about to tell her to call him Connor. He didn't.

His jaw shifted; he glanced toward the far side of the pool.

She felt an irrational loss.

He leaned down, opened a small cooler beside him and brought out an icy bottle of spring water. "Want one?"

"No, thanks." The refusal had been automatic. She'd trained herself to rebuff any overture that could possibly lead to familiarity.

But as she watched him open the bottle and take a swallow, she realized how dry her mouth had become since she'd finished the syrupy Punch Cola. She knew she had to drink plenty of water. Since her visit to his office, she'd taken extra care to drink more fluids and had noticed a definite improvement. The dizziness came less frequently.

In the chair beside her, Dr. Connor Wade laid back his head and shut his eyes. His silky hair and deeply tanned skin glistened in the afternoon sun, emitting a natural male scent that mingled appealingly with suntan lotion.

She closed her eyes to better savor his scent, and then found it difficult to reopen them. If she didn't do something to rouse herself, she'd be nodding off to sleep.

Forcing herself to act, she rose from the lounge chair and walked to the pool. The sudden rise brought on a wave of dizziness, and heat rushed up at her from the hot concrete. She grabbed hold of the pool's chrome ladder to steady herself. Below her, children squealed, splashed and kicked in a churning mass. She hadn't the strength to venture into the merry fray.

Instead she held on to the ladder railing, knelt at

the side of the pool and dipped up the sparkling, cold water in her cupped hand. Closing her eyes, she tilted back her head and poured the water over herself, drenching her face, neck and shoulders in a magnificent rush of coolness.

She indulged again in the refreshing bite of the cold against her heated skin, this time ladling the water onto her throat and chest. The coldness sluiced down her breasts and arms, raising chill bumps and tightening her nipples to a sensitive hardness.

The sensuality of it brought to mind Connor Wade, and without further thought, she peered at him.

His eyes were no longer closed.

He was watching her. Intensely so. His powerful upper body was now angled forward, his muscled forearms resting across his knees. His stare followed the trickle of water down her face, throat and arms...then lingered on her peaking breasts.

The hunger in his gaze took her breath away.

She averted her eyes and stood on legs that trembled. Her swimsuit concealed more than did many of the others here today, but the filmy beige fabric molded to her curves like shrink-wrap, especially when wet. She felt wickedly exposed.

Because *he* watched her.

And in the most intimate parts of her body, she thrilled to the titillating knowledge.

Flushed with inner heat, she concentrated on returning to her chair. She avoided looking at him as she approached, though she couldn't have been more conscious of him if he'd reached out and grazed her nipples with his hands.

She settled into the lounge chair and closed her eyes, but each beat of her heart jostled her back to awareness of Connor. Was he still watching?

She had to know. She stole a peek from beneath her lashes.

He wasn't. He stared off in an unfocused way, his lips a tight, thin line, a muscle flexing in his jaw. "That ought to be illegal," he rasped.

Heat flared in her stomach. The chemistry that had always simmered between them suddenly felt explosive.

And dangerous.

Get away from him, an inner voice cried. But she couldn't leave. She had to watch Jeffrey and Timmy!

"Hi, Dr. Wade."

Out of nowhere, two lanky teenage girls appeared in ruffled bikinis and dropped down onto towels near Connor. "You were right about my brother's flu," remarked one of them, her braces gleaming as she grinned. "It went away the next day."

Sarah whispered a prayer of gratitude for the girls' friendly intrusion. Although the pool area was teeming with people, she'd felt virtually alone with the man beside her.

"Oooh, gross!" the other girl squealed. "Don't talk about the flu." She swatted her friend with a glossy magazine, and they both giggled. With a fetching smile for Connor, she asked, "Don't you get sick of seeing all those sick people?"

Amused to see him cornered, Sarah wilted against the chair, glad for the chance to compose herself. Why did her body hum with such tense sexuality whenever he was near?

The girls asked him how fast his boat could go and what he'd named his horses. He uttered brief but amiable replies.

Sarah listened to his voice rather than his words. That alone stimulated her in a disturbing way. She tried to tune out the sound and found herself giving way to the drowsiness.

She forced her eyes open and searched for Jeffrey and Timmy. They were tossing a ball with other kids in the water.

"Hey, Dr. Wade, I'll read your horoscope," volunteered the girl with the magazine. "What's your sign?"

"Leo."

The girl read aloud, and Sarah's eyes drifted closed again. Leo, he'd said. She imagined a great, tawny lion poised beside her, sleek and muscled, with a low, sexy growl...and the most dangerous hazel eyes in the jungle....

"I think you should read Ms. Flowers's horoscope, too," the man beast beside her purred in that velvet-deep growl of his.

"Ms. Flowers?"

Sarah jerked herself out of a dream state and lifted her head from the chair, struggling to focus her gaze.

The two girls were shyly eyeing her. She hadn't introduced herself to anyone at the pool, or in town. From the surreptitious glances of nearby sunbathers, she realized she'd stirred up curiosity.

Connor tipped her a smile, though she sensed it

cost him some effort. "What's your sign, Ms. Flowers?"

Her sign? She didn't know it. Dismay flushed through her until she realized that no one would know whether she was right or not. Choosing one, she murmured, "Gemini."

The girl read from her magazine about big money, a high-powered career and a daring romance. Sarah smiled her thanks and rested her head back again. Apparently she wasn't a Gemini.

The sun beat down hotter, if that were possible, and her drowsiness grew overpowering. The Punch Cola hadn't worked at all, she mused. In fact, she felt as if she'd been drugged with sedatives.

She wondered if the caffeine could be having the opposite effect than the one she'd expected. A memory stirred in the hazy recesses of her mind: She couldn't drink more than one cup of coffee, or it would put her to sleep....

"Funny," came Connor's voice from far away. "I thought your birthday was in mid-September. Wouldn't that make you a Virgo?"

She frowned...or thought she did, if her face muscles had cooperated. Why would he think he knew her birthday? Even *she* didn't know her birthday.

In answer to her unasked question, he leaned closer and whispered, "From your medical chart. September fifteenth, I believe you wrote."

She knew she should be alarmed by what he'd said, but she couldn't quite grasp why. The humming around her had turned into a deeper drone, and the warm, red darkness lured her into sleep.

"Sarah?" Connor's voice reached her through some tunnel. "Sarah." He touched her arm, but she couldn't respond with more than a groan.

In a distant part of her, panic sparked. Jeffrey and Timmy needed her, but the sleepiness had grown too heavy to resist.

"Promise me you'll go to him if you need help." Annie had said that, about Connor Wade. But Annie hadn't known how vulnerable she could be with him. How the sensuality could blaze so quickly beyond her control.

She slipped deeper into the darkness.

Marshaling the little strength she had left, she blindly reached out and touched the muscled arm beside her. "Connor," she whispered, her eyelids fluttering in a vain attempt to open. "Can't stay awake. Can't...watch...the boys."

She wasn't entirely sure the words had even left her mouth when he rose from his chair and leaned over her. Laying his hand against her forehead, he asked questions about how she felt.

"Sleepy," she murmured. "Just want to sleep."

"I'm going to listen to your breathing," he told her. Before she fully understood, he'd pressed his ear and silky, fragrant hair against her throat. If she hadn't been so terribly lethargic, she might have stopped breathing altogether....

He gripped her wrist and checked her pulse, his fingers strong and firm, then patted cold water against her face. Pressing a bottle to her lips, he instructed, "Drink."

She obeyed. Cool, wonderful water.

Through a muffling haze, she heard him give orders to someone about Timmy and Jeffrey. Moments later, he leaned close again, his scent and his nearness oddly comforting. "You can't sleep here for long in the sun, Sarah. Can you walk?"

She nodded, hoping it was true. Strong arms helped her stand, bracketed her waist, then braced her against a lean, hard body. She concentrated on taking each step and keeping her eyes reasonably open, although everything looked blurred.

Connor asked her if she'd been getting any sleep lately.

She admitted she hadn't.

When they reached the parking lot, he stopped and swept her feet out from under her. He was carrying her, she realized.

Nestled against the muscled wall of his chest, near the forceful beating of his heart, she tucked her face into the curve of his neck and gave in to the persistent darkness.

CONNOR CURSED HIMSELF long and hard. He'd promised to leave her alone, and what was he doing? Carrying her to his car!

It wasn't as if she needed medical attention. He'd determined that she wasn't in immediate danger of dehydration and that she hadn't fainted. She was merely sleeping—normal, healthy sleep that was long overdue.

After his anger had somewhat cooled, he allowed himself a little justification: He couldn't have left her lying in the sun. And she *had* asked for his help.

Never had he been so gratified by a request for help.

He'd taken care of her immediate concern by

asking the two teenage girls to escort Jeffrey and Timmy to Lorna. He'd watched as they ushered the boys to the tennis court where they'd found her. Lorna hadn't looked happy about the interruption...or at the sight of him leaving with her maid/cook/baby-sitter.

Too bad.

Since he'd overheard the cold way she'd spoken to Sarah last night, he'd seen Lorna in a new light. The elegance he'd admired since high school now seemed more like arrogance, and her warmth seemed shallow. He wished he hadn't asked her to this evening's charity dance. He'd take her, but only because he'd committed to it.

Wasting little time on thoughts of Lorna, he returned his attention to Sarah. She apparently hadn't been sleeping lately. He wanted to know why. He wanted to know quite a few things about her.

He'd already learned one—how she felt in his arms. The silkiness of her skin against his, the voluptuous crush of her breast against his chest, the enticing heaviness of her hair as it cascaded down his arm and shoulder.

He'd known she would feel good. He hadn't known *how* good.

He settled her into the reclining passenger seat of his Jaguar sports coupe. She tried to lift her head. It looked like quite a struggle. "Timmy and Jeffrey..."

"They're with their mother."

She groaned, as if she wasn't too happy to hear that. "I have to talk to her. I have to tell that I—"

"I'll call her. You relax."

Laying her head back down, she whispered an apology for being so sleepy. He assured her he didn't mind, brushed a silky tendril away from her half-closed eyes and urged her to sleep.

By the time he'd taken his place behind the wheel, dialed his cell phone and left a message on Lorna's answering machine, Sarah had shifted onto her side, rested her head on her arm and dozed off into a deep, silent slumber.

He tried not to look at her as he drove. She'd folded her elegant legs up against her. Her provocative bathing suit molded itself perfectly to her rounded backside and bared a long, sleek expanse of hip, thigh and calf.

He forced himself to breathe. And to stay on the road.

Slowly he drove down the narrow, hilly streets of town, past the awning-shaded shops on the square, the ornate gazebo in the park and the turbulent waterfall at the Main Street Bridge.

Where should he take her?

Since she wasn't sick, he saw no reason to install her in the clinic where he'd have to sit idly beside her for hours. He could drop her off at Lorna's house, of course, but she'd be woken up and working in no time. Besides, if he were to be honest with himself, he'd admit that he wanted to stay with her. To make sure she wasn't disturbed, he rationalized.

He considered taking her to his house. To his bed, where she could sleep in comfort. Thinking of her there filled his gut with heat. He hadn't lost his mind entirely, though. She probably wouldn't appreciate waking up to find herself in his house, in his bed. It wasn't worth the risk of losing whatever trust she had in him...not when she'd finally asked him for help.

He drove her instead to a nearby grassy spot shaded by cottonwood trees, high on a plateau that overlooked Juneberry Lake. A smattering of other couples reclined on blankets a few dozen feet below them.

This, he decided, should do just fine. He wasn't entirely alone with her here, yet they would have some privacy. No one would bother them.

Juneberry Lake was a place for lovers.

The heavy scent of springtime grasses, wild plum and lilac carried to him on the breeze. The shade of the cottonwood trees pleasantly curbed the heat of the afternoon. Birds sang, chirped and bantered in the surrounding woods.

Stretched out comfortably on a blanket he'd kept on hand for roadside medical emergencies, he propped himself up on an elbow beside her and watched her sleep. He'd covered her as best he could with his chambray shirt, mostly to preserve what little sanity he had left. With much of her body curled beneath it, she looked soft, sweet, and altogether too kissable.

His blood stirred.

Did the woman have any idea how she affected him?

He'd never forget what she'd done to him at the pool, with her Gypsy-dark hair shining halfway to her narrow waist and her long, smooth legs wickedly bare. Though he knew every facet of the human body and could probably construct a model in his sleep, hers somehow bewitched him, with every curve flowing mystically into the next.

He'd had a damn hard time keeping his eyes off her.

Then she'd splashed that cold water over herself and turned to him with a sultry stare. The stare alone had made his mouth go dry. When the wet fabric of her swimsuit had outlined her breasts in intimate detail, he'd nearly come out of his chair.

She was sexier than sin and lit fires in his blood, but she had an innocence about her, too. A sweet, irresistible innocence that tied his insides in knots.

It wasn't wise to want her so much.

She rolled toward him, dislodging the shirt from her shoulders. The sun had kissed them with an appealing golden glow, and he had to force himself not to touch her.

Growing restless, she shifted again. Her dark, delicate brows knit together. A groan escaped her, then a whimper.

A bad dream?

Her breathing quickened. Her brow furrowed. "No," she whispered, her eyes tightly closed. "No-o-o!"

He rubbed her arm to soothe her. "Shh. You're okay."

She continued to thrash about until she sobbed. Shaken by her anguish, Connor pulled her firmly into his arms and murmured incoherent sounds of assurance.

Apparently something traumatic had frightened or upset her. What? Something had sent her running to this small, out-of-the-way town where she kept strictly to herself, working in a job far below her potential, lying even to doctors about her history.

He wished she'd trust him. He wanted to help her. And to protect her. And to take away the fear he sensed was at least partially responsible for the way she held herself beyond his reach.

"Jack!" she cried in an anguished whisper. "Jack."

Connor froze, his heart standing still. *Jack?* Swallowing against a suddenly tight throat, he stroked her hair and shoulders. The tension gradually left her body and her trembling ceased.

Jack. The name settled like a lump in his stomach. Who was Jack and why was she dreaming about him? *What* was she dreaming about him? He couldn't be sure if she'd said the name in fear, in sadness or in longing. Was he someone she'd run from, or someone she desperately missed?

The questions dug deep into his gut, reminding him of all the reasons he'd sworn to keep his distance from her.

He continued to hold her, anyway. And to stroke her hair, her shoulders and the long, slender curve of her back, closing his eyes to better savor the silky textures.

She cuddled to him, molding her warm, firm body to his with the easiness of a lover. Did she think he was someone else? Even as he wondered, sensual warmth sparked and radiated within him.

She felt so damn right in his arms. He ached to run his hands all over her, beyond the boundaries; to wake her with kisses, strip off their swimsuits and make sweet, hot love to her.

Who the hell was Jack?

Whoever he was, he wasn't here now. And no one, but no one, would stop him from holding her for as long as he could.

THE GROAN DISRUPTED HER dream. And it was such a lovely dream, too—of being held, stroked and cuddled by some strong, sexy man until she purred and arched and rubbed herself against him.

"Sarah."

She couldn't tell if the deep, gruff whisper was part of her dream or not. Choosing to ignore it, she entwined her legs with the hairy, muscular ones beside her. Mmm...wonderful.

The groan came again, sounding tortured this time. Arms tightened around her, and a whisper tingled across her ear, "Sarah, sweetheart, you're killing me."

Killing him? That didn't quite mesh with her dream.

Her eyelids lifted halfway open. She wasn't particularly surprised to find a sinewy arm lodged beneath her head and her cheek pressed against a biceps. Her palm rested on a muscular chest with her fingers woven through its silky curls.

This was all part of her dream...wasn't it?

Suddenly unsure, she opened her eyes the rest of the way. She found herself gazing into a deeply tanned, handsome face with hooded hazel eyes only inches from hers.

She recognized him immediately, of course—the man who held her so closely; the man whose legs were twined with hers.

Connor Wade.

He'd rescued her at the club and walked her to

his car. No, carried her. Confusion dazed her. What had happened after that?

With his tousled hair and heavy-lidded eyes, he looked as if he, too, had been sleeping and recently awakened. She wore nothing but a swimsuit, she realized. Neither did he. They lay skin to skin, face-to-face...and he was gazing at her with a sexual hunger that kindled a slow, languid heat within her.

"Before you say a word," he murmured hoarsely, "there's something I really, really have to do." His hand curled around her nape and he leaned in closer.

She knew what he wanted. She wanted it, too. A kiss. Just one. She angled her face for it.

He brushed his mouth slowly across hers, the tip of his tongue gliding velvet-soft against the inner swell of her lips. Wetting them. Parting them. He followed through with another lingering pass, penetrating deeper this time.

A sound of arousal rose in her throat, and she slid her palms around his hot, muscled shoulders.

He groaned, pressed her down onto her back and moved his hand to her jaw. Lodging his thumb against her face, he made slow, intricate love to her mouth.

Desire coursed in hot, wicked currents to the far reaches of her body. She felt alive, wonderfully alive, as she hadn't for so long. She reveled in the mindless pleasure spilling through her, wanting more of his heat, his mouth, his body.

But the kiss soon ended, and he pulled back. Though his hazel eyes burned into hers, she saw

hesitation there, too. "Sarah," he asked in a doubtful whisper, "are you fully awake?"

She nodded, wanting only to melt back into his
kiss.

"And you know it's me? Connor."

"Connor," she acknowledged softly. Who else
would it be?

It was then, though, that her thought process
kicked back into gear. Of course it was Connor...but what was she doing with him? She had
no business kissing him, or lying half-naked in his
arms! Her eyes widened in alarm. "What are we
doing?" she cried in a strangled whisper. "What
the *hell* are we doing?"

He shut his eyes as if she'd slapped him. Shifting
out of her embrace, he settled onto his back and
stared at the sky.

She sat up and looked wildly around her, panic
replacing the heat she'd felt only moments before.
"For heaven's sake, where are we?"

"Juneberry Lake."

"Juneberry Lake!" She glanced down at him in
confusion. "But, why? You helped me walk out of
the club, I remember, and you carried me to your
car. Then you...you brought me to some secluded
spot by a lake?" she deduced incredulously.

"It's not all that secluded." His words were dry,
clipped and only slightly defensive. "There's a
good number of people at the foot of this hill."

She glanced down the hill. "I don't see anyone."

He sat up and looked for himself. Dismay re-
placed his surliness. He glanced at his watch. "It's
late. We've got to go."

"What time is it?" From the low, golden slant of

the sun over the surrounding mountains and the slight chill that had pervaded the mountain air, she knew the hour had grown late. Five o'clock, or maybe even six. Either way, she'd been away from her job for far too long.

"It's almost seven."

"Seven!" The pronouncement stunned her.

"I should have woken you sooner," he admitted, his face taut with self-reproach, "but I fell asleep, too. Guess I haven't been sleeping very well myself." He slanted her a glance that somehow blamed her. The heat behind the glance reminded her of their kiss.

She looked away, shaken by the sensual feelings he roused so easily in her.

"Here. Put this on. It's getting chilly." He held a man's blue chambray shirt open in readiness for her.

Grateful for a cover over her skimpy swimsuit and for the warmth the shirt provided, she slipped her arms into the large, rolled-up sleeves. His masculine scent pleasantly embraced her as she wriggled into the soft folds of the shirt.

He assisted her in the effort, curtly tugging the fabric into place around her, freeing her hair from beneath the collar and fastening each button. As he worked, his unsmiling gaze traveled slowly upward to roam across her face.

She grew too breathless in the intimacy of that gaze, too aware of his long, deft fingers working between her breasts. Her hands caught his halfway down. "I'll do it," she whispered.

She half hoped he'd nudge her hands away, unbutton the shirt, tug it off her shoulders, tumble her down to the blanket....

But slowly he withdrew his hands.

Tearing her gaze from his, she took over the task of buttoning the shirt, dazed by her intoxicating attraction to him. She should be focusing on the crisis she'd soon face. She had no doubt there would be one.

"We've been gone all afternoon," she remarked, needing to break the heart-thudding silence between them, "and I didn't even tell Lorna I was leaving."

"I told her."

"She knows I'm with you?"

"After our exit from the pool, I'm sure everyone does." He rose to his feet and held out his hand to help her up.

She took it, relishing its steadiness and strength. "Then the only way she won't have my head," she predicted direly, "is if she personally sees me having a major blood transfusion tonight in your clinic."

"That's an idea." He kept her hand loosely in his, even after she'd risen. "You wouldn't mind, would you? Might be the only excuse she'll accept for us being this late. Of course, I'd have to give my own blood."

They shared a mere suggestion of a smile. Slowly he relinquished her hand, swept the blanket up from the ground and ushered her toward his gleaming black Jaguar. "I was supposed to pick her up at six."

Sarah stared at him, absorbing his words, then shut her eyes. The dance! How could she have forgotten about the dance? She should have been baby-sitting the boys by now. And Connor should have been wearing some elegant tux, with Lorna grandstanding at his side.

Lorna would be furious.

"I'm sorry that I ruined your date," Sarah said miserably, mortified by the trouble she had caused. And yet, in a secret part of her heart, she hoped she *had* ruined their date...which mortified her all the more.

With his sleek, muscular back to her, he tossed the blanket into his car and muttered something unintelligible. He couldn't know, of course, what Lorna's anger would mean for her. No one but Annie knew how desperately Sarah needed the job... and Annie would be gone for another couple of weeks yet.

Sarah's anxiety mounted. She'd have nowhere to stay if Lorna fired her, and no money to tide her over until she found another job. How could she even look for another job? She had no car, phone or references...not even a social security number.

Connor crossed his muscled arms, settled against his low, sleek sports car and studied her. "Don't worry about Lorna. I'll call and explain what happened. We'll stop by my house. I'll shower and change." He shrugged—a nonchalant, masculine movement of his broad shoulders. "We'll just be a little late, that's all."

Sarah tossed her head in silent scorn. "How will you explain being so late? That we were sleeping together and lost track of the time?"

A corner of his mouth shot up and an enchanting

groove deepened beside it. "Maybe I won't put it quite that way."

She let out a harried breath, raked a heavy wave of hair from her face and paced. "It won't matter what you tell her. The damage has been done. She's going to fire me."

He watched the sway of her hips as she passed by him—a fact she noticed through the car's side mirror. "I don't see why," he replied gruffly. "I warned her last night that you needed a few days of bed rest. It's her fault as much as anyone's for not insisting you take off work at least one day."

"It really wasn't Lorna's fault. She didn't drag me out of bed." Pacing back toward him, she threw a sheepish glance his way. "I...I guess I should have listened to you."

"Damn right." He looked a little too pleased at her admission.

"Of course, I probably wouldn't have fallen asleep at the pool if it hadn't been for that Punch Cola."

"Punch Cola? You mean that liquid caffeine they sell as a soft drink?"

"I thought it might help me wake up." Feeling somewhat abashed by the disapproval in his stare, she stopped her pacing and leaned against the car beside him. "Guess it had the opposite effect on me."

"Caffeine puts you to sleep?" His eyebrow lifted with interest. "Hmm. That's rare. I've read case studies involving that reaction, but—" He paused, and his tawny brows converged. "If you know caffeine puts you to sleep, why did you think the cola would wake you up?"

Nervousness flushed through her at the question. She searched for a plausible explanation. "I'd forgotten how caffeine puts me to sleep. I mean, I don't drink coffee or cola very often, and never very much of it." Which had been the truth…at least, for the past seven weeks since her accident.

"You're twenty-five years old and haven't had much coffee or cola?"

Her gaze snapped back to his. "You remembered my age from that medical chart, didn't you?"

"That's right."

"What did you do?" she cried in exasperation. "Memorize the whole blasted thing?"

"So what if I did? It's part of my job."

"To remember my birth date?"

"Do you remember it, Sarah?" There was no escaping his keen gaze. "Do you remember what date you wrote down as your birthday?"

She didn't. She hadn't paid much attention to the date she'd randomly chosen. But she thought back to what he'd said at the pool, just before she'd nodded off to sleep. "September fifteenth."

"Wrong. September sixteenth."

She blanched in speechless dismay. He'd tricked her!

"I don't understand why you'd lie about a thing like that," he rebuked, "or anything else on a medical form…and yet, everything on yours was a lie, wasn't it?"

"Not a lie!" She felt unreasonably offended by the harsh term. After a moment, though, she hesitantly allowed, "Maybe all the information wasn't exactly *precise.…*"

"Why not?"

When she failed to answer, his mouth thinned. The silence between them grew tense. "Keep your secrets, then," he said in a low, hoarse rumble, "if that makes you feel safer. But understand this, Sarah." His stare pinned her against the car. "No matter what kind of trouble you're in or what you're running from, you can tell me. I won't do anything you don't want me to. I won't hurt you."

Her throat closed up. She felt like crying. Should she tell him about her amnesia? The truth couldn't make him any more suspicious of her than he was right now.

She wanted to trust him. She *did* trust him. That fact alone frightened her. She'd trusted foolishly before, with disastrous results....

While she searched her mind for how she knew this, Connor turned away and reached through the open window of his car for the cell phone. The warmth had gone from his expression. He now looked dark and shuttered.

A stranger.

The choice had been hers.

"Connor," she whispered on an impulse, catching hold of his arm.

His muscles hardened beneath her fingers as he swung his gaze back to hers with a stern, silent question.

An odd tenderness welled up in her. She couldn't forget his kindness today, or the time he'd devoted to her. Or the way his kiss had blessed her with a sweet, vibrant taste of life—maybe the only taste she'd have in a long, long time to come.

Her lips curved and her eyes misted. "Before

things get any worse with Lorna and I get side-tracked, I...I want to thank you for helping me today." She swallowed a sudden thickness in her throat. "For taking me from the club and staying with me. I know you had better things to do with your time."

The guardedness left his face and his eyes darkened with a powerful intensity. "I can't think of a damn thing better than holding you all afternoon. Unless it's holding you all night."

Sensual longing engulfed her. His dark solemn face filled her vision. The promise of his kiss overwhelmed her with need.

A sudden ringing of a cell phone erupted between them. Startled, she drew back.

Connor uttered a soft curse, swept a heated gaze across her mouth and brought the cell phone to his ear. After a brusque greeting, he stiffened and turned away. "Lorna. I was just about to call you. Sorry I'm late. If you still want to go, I can stop by my—"

He broke off abruptly, and a moment passed. "You called me? I didn't hear the phone. Guess I left it in the car." He fell silent again, and his gaze met Sarah's. "Yeah, she's still with me."

Sarah caught her bottom lip between her teeth.

A frown gradually formed on his face. "Hold on, there, Lorna. We've been dealing with a health-related issue, which—if you'll remember—I warned you about last night." He glared into the steadily increasing darkness. "*You* made the choice to send her to the pool with the kids after I made it perfectly clear—"

He paused. A subtle flush seeped beneath his

tan. "Juneberry Lake? Well, yeah, I suppose we were, but…" He shut his eyes and bowed his head. In the next instant, he brought it back up. "Actually, it's none of your business what we were doing there. I've apologized for being late, and I— Lorna?"

Clenching his jaw, he slung the cell phone through the open window into his car. Bracing herself for the worst, Sarah waited in dread for the news he'd surely deliver.

After a grim, silent moment, he turned to her. She sensed anger simmering within him, yet his gaze conveyed his regret. "I'm sorry, Sarah. You were right. Lorna fired you. She's, uh, leaving your suitcase on her front porch. You can pick up your final paycheck next Friday."

5

THEY FOUND HER SUITCASE on the wide, columned front porch of Lorna's Colonial mansion—one suitcase with a folded note taped to its handle. Nothing more. He'd expected considerably more. She had, after all, been living here.

The sight of that lone suitcase somehow made Connor feel worse than he already did. The look on Sarah's face had told him how much the job meant to her. He couldn't understand why. He felt sure she could find a better one. She didn't seem to realize that, though.

Not that she'd shared her feelings with him. She'd barely said a word since they'd left the lake.

He followed her up the walkway to the porch, where she stooped beside the suitcase and unzipped a small, almost-hidden side compartment. Reaching in, she retrieved a slim stack of cash. Flipping through bills, she bit her lip and tucked the money into her purse.

"Is it all there?"

"Of course," she murmured. "I never suspected it wouldn't be. I just couldn't remember exactly how much I'd saved."

From her air of subdued desperation, he guessed it wasn't enough. Surely, those few bills couldn't be *all* her savings. She'd certainly have a bank account to draw on and a few credit cards at her disposal.

His gut told him otherwise.

"Do you have a car here?" he asked.

"No."

She detached the note taped to the handle of her suitcase, and he read the emotions in her cloud-gray eyes. Anger, though not nearly enough of it to suit him. Remorse, which shouldn't have been there at all. But the dominant emotion looked like fear.

Why should losing a temporary job cause her *fear?*

Her steadfast refusal to vent her feelings only fanned his anger at both Lorna and himself. He believed that Lorna had acted out of spite. And he, damn his soul, had acted out of self-gratification. He should have dropped Sarah off at Lorna's after leaving the club, but he'd wanted to stay with her. He should have watched the time, but he'd gotten lost in the wonder of holding her. He'd fallen asleep with the scent of her in his nostrils and the feel of her in his arms…a pleasure too intense to regret, even now.

Calling himself the worst of names, he grabbed the suitcase from beside her and carried it to his car.

Sarah remained on the porch and read the note. When she'd finished, her chin came up and she pivoted to rap on Lorna's door.

Lorna, however, didn't answer the brisk knocking, just as she hadn't answered her phone when Connor had tried to call. Squaring her shoulders,

Sarah kept her head high as she strode down the walkway from the mansion's porch.

From his watchful stance beside the car, Connor noticed how pale she had grown. "What was in the note?" he demanded, fully intending to be told.

She hesitated, but after a glance at his face, let out a weary breath and shrugged, as if it mattered little to her what the note had said. "Her reasons for firing me."

"What were they?"

Though she tried to remain impassive, telltale color seeped into her face. "Leaving her children unsupervised at the club while I…" She paused, as if trying to find the right words.

He snatched the note from her hand and read it for himself. She'd left out the part where Lorna had accused her of "throwing herself at men," and her report that the entire community was "shocked and dismayed by her behavior."

Connor crumpled the note in his fist and glared at the house. "I'll 'shock and dismay' her, all right." He started toward it.

Sarah stepped in his way to stop him. "I appreciate your support, Connor, but this isn't your battle to fight. There's been a simple misunderstanding. I can see how she'd arrive at the conclusion she has. We walked out of the club with your arm around me, and she apparently learned that we spent the afternoon at Juneberry Lake. If you care about your relationship with her, you'll wait until tomorrow when she's cooled down and explain that there's nothing between us."

"But that would be a lie." He held her gaze the way he wanted to hold her. "Whether you're willing to do anything about it or not...there *is* something between us, Sarah."

A breathless silence overtook them.

A boyish shout disrupted that silence. "Sarah!" A small, barefoot figure darted from the shadows at the side of the mansion. "Sarah, wait!"

"Timmy." She turned toward him and gaped at the pajama-clad boy running barefoot down the long, rolling driveway. "It's getting chilly out here. You should have shoes on, or slippers."

"Sarah!" he wailed. To Connor's surprise, the holy terror of the peewee baseball league threw his chubby arms around her knees. "*Please* don't go!"

"Hey, hey, what's this all about?" she asked in a gentle, almost-teasing tone as she tousled his dark, reddish hair. "I haven't seen you run that fast since you made your big home run."

Flushed and panting, he regarded her dolefully from beneath shaggy bangs. "My mom's giving Tofu away, and now she's giving you away, too. It's not fair. Don't go, Sarah. Jeffrey and me, we want to keep you!" His voice had choked up.

She dropped to her knees with a tender smile. "Oh, Timmy, I wish I could stay. But I... Well, I have to find another job."

"No, no... Then you won't watch cartoons with us, or play."

"We might get the chance to have fun together again. I might even come to some of your ball games...if I stay in town."

"*If I stay in town.*" Connor tensed at that.

"Promise?" Timmy implored her. "Cross your heart, hope to die, stick a hundred needles in your eye?"

She winced with comic exaggeration, but held her hand up and uttered a vow. "If I'm in town, I promise to come to as many of your games as I can. Now, you'd better get back to the house. *The Gruesome Twosome* show will be coming on TV soon."

"*The Gruesome Twosome!*" he exclaimed with boyish vigor. "I better get the remote before Jeffrey does." He took off running. But then he stopped, turned back to her and dug something out of his pajama pocket. "I almost forgot. I brought these for you." He cupped his hand over hers and dropped his offering into her palm. "In case you want to play when I'm not there."

She closed her hand around the gift, murmured her thanks and hugged him—really hugged him, as a mother might hug her son. Timmy tolerated it for a moment, then pulled away, leaving her with a shout of, "See ya later, alligator!"

"After a while, crocodile!" she called back. She slowly stood and stared in the direction he'd taken until they heard the side screen-door slam. Wordlessly, then, she turned to Connor, who guided her with a light hand at her waist to his car.

When she'd settled into the passenger seat, he paused in the open doorway. "What did he give you?"

She smiled up at him with shiny, liquid eyes. "Army Men." Unfurling her hand, she showed him. Her smile slipped a little. She turned her head abruptly away, closed her hand and held it against her heart. "His favorite ones," she croaked.

He fell in love with her then, or maybe he just realized at that moment how totally, overwhelmingly, he'd already fallen. He wanted to take her home with him and make love to her for the rest of his life...not just to her lush, slender body, but to the woman behind the tear-shiny eyes and tender smile.

He understood perfectly what Timmy had meant.

Connor, too, wanted to keep her. Badly.

It was craziness, of course. As crazy as his father's obsession with the "natural way" and the mountains he'd considered paradise. As crazy as his mother's belief in yin and yang, the zodiac and the curative powers of flute music. As crazy as their needless deaths.

Falling in love was the craziest of all—especially with Sarah Flowers. He knew nothing about her other than the fact that she'd lied on her medical form, ran away from him whenever she could, turned him inside out with her kiss and whispered another man's name in her sleep.

He was in trouble. Deep trouble. He'd lost his head and he'd have to find it. But she needed him at the moment, and he would, by God, help her.

"Let's go get some supper," he suggested. "It's seven-thirty. You've got to be as hungry as I am."

"Thanks, but I'd better register in a hotel. Would you mind dropping me off at the nearest one?"

"A hotel? I thought you'd want to go to Annie's. She *is* your cousin, isn't she?"

That wary look entered her eyes again and made his muscles tense up. "She's away on a camping trip. She won't be home for another couple weeks."

He pursed his lips and drove for a while in speculative silence. "The only hotel nearby is Beck's Lodge at the fishing camp. I have no idea what your financial situation is, but it'll cost you around a hundred dollars a night to stay there."

Fear flickered again in her eyes, but she didn't reply.

"Are you planning to find another job here," he persisted, maybe a little too gruffly, "or leave town?"

"I...I really can't say."

"'Can't say?'" His anger surged. He cut the wheel sharply and turned down the road to his house in simmering, tight-lipped silence.

"Connor?" She gripped the armrest and glanced at him as he turned into his tree-lined driveway and brought the car to a sudden halt.

"I'm not going to beg you to trust me." He pulled the key out of the ignition, removed it from his key ring and tossed it into her lap. "Take the car. Go to the hotel."

In startled surprise, she caught the key between her knees to keep it from falling.

He reached across her to the glove compartment and retrieved his wallet. Flipping it open, he withdrew a credit card, which he also tossed at her. "Use this to pay for the room. If you decide to leave town, you can rent a car with it. Call my office and leave a message where I can pick up mine."

She blinked at him in disbelief. "You're trusting me with your car and your credit card? But...you don't even know me!"

He turned to her with a glare that was both angry and intimate. "I know you, Sarah. I just don't know a damn thing *about* you. And it seems you want it that way." He slung open his door and got out.

By the time she'd opened hers, he'd crossed a grassy yard with a few long strides and climbed the stone steps of a quaint log cabin. The night had grown surprisingly cold after the heat of the day, and she shivered in his thin chambray shirt as she followed him.

"Connor!" she cried, shaken by his anger. "Please, wait."

He stopped on the porch and regarded her in chilly silence.

"I can't take your car, or your credit card."

His expression darkened into a definite scowl. "Why not?"

"To start with, I can't drive." She wrapped her arms around herself for warmth and comfort. "I don't have a license."

"What?" he exclaimed, incredulous.

"And I doubt if they'd let me use your credit card. I...I don't have any identification."

He stared at her.

She climbed the few steps and held out his key and credit card.

He took her hand instead. Slowly, insistently, he pulled her to him. His arms came around her with a welcoming warmth. Sighing in frustration, he settled his beard-stubbled jaw against her temple. He didn't ask a single question.

"You were right," she admitted, no longer afraid to tell him. *He'd been willing to let her go.* She had no idea why that revelation should make her feel so free, but it did. The knowledge that he'd allow her to leave him put to rest an uneasiness that had been growing from the first time she'd sensed his desire. "I lied to you."

He didn't speak or move. He simply held her there in the chilly, moonlit shadows of his front porch.

"But before I tell you the truth, I want you to promise me something." She leaned back in his arms just enough to meet his somber gaze. "Promise you won't do anything about this. Nothing at all. You've got to leave the matter entirely up to me."

He frowned, as if he might refuse. His gaze intensified, and after a moment, he reluctantly uttered, "Okay. I promise."

"Cross your heart, hope to die, stick a hundred needles in your eye?"

That coaxed a smile to his eyes, if not to his lips. "Don't push it."

Her heart felt infinitely lighter. They shared another gaze; a calmer, deeper one.

"I told you that I suffered no memory loss after the head trauma," she began, "but I did. Quite a bit, actually. I, uh, can't remember anything about my past." She swallowed a sudden dryness in her throat. "I don't know who I am."

THE FIRE DANCED AND crackled in the gray-stone hearth beside them as they lounged on large floor pillows and a handwoven rug. They'd finished the ham sandwiches he'd made with delectable homemade bread and now nursed glasses of light, dry wine.

She'd told him everything she remembered, including her certainty that someone had been chasing her before the accident. Someone dangerous.

"So you lied to the doctors in the hospital," he

summarized. "You told them your memory had returned because you were afraid they'd keep you there and word would get out about your amnesia."

"That's right. I was afraid that whoever had been chasing me would find me, and I—" a light shiver of fear went through her "—I felt very strongly that I was in danger. I wanted to get away without leaving too much of a trail."

"And that was why you kept the amnesia a secret from me and everyone else in town. You were afraid word would reach the wrong ears."

"That, and the fact that people don't trust a stranger who claims to have amnesia. I heard Annie's husband tell her he doesn't trust me. I couldn't afford to have everyone in town suspicious or I'd never have gotten a job."

He studied her intently for a long while. "You dream about it, don't you?" he asked softly. "About being chased, I mean."

She glanced at him in surprise. "Yes. How did you know?"

He shrugged. "A guess. You had a nightmare this afternoon while you slept."

"I did?" She could hardly believe it. "The nightmares usually wake me."

"This one probably would have," he said, "if I hadn't been holding you." Sensuality tingled through her at the huskiness of his voice and the directness of his gaze. "Your fear might be a reaction to the head trauma, Sarah, but if there *is* any basis for it, I won't let anyone hurt you."

His protectiveness touched her, but at the same time, filled her with anxiety. She'd already dissuaded him from calling the authorities to report her amnesia. She'd had to firmly remind him of his promise to do nothing.

Would he keep that promise?

She worried not only for herself now, but also for him. *He'd be hurt.* Physically hurt. *Any man who tried to help her would be hurt.* She knew it with a certainty that frightened her.

"The fear is probably groundless," she assured him as convincingly as she could, wishing she'd never mentioned it, "but I'd rather wait until more memories come back before I publicize my amnesia." She stared down into her wineglass. "I'm not ready for some stranger to step forward and...and claim me."

"Claim you," he repeated. Their gazes locked again. "My God. You might be married."

Slowly, reluctantly, she nodded.

"But you weren't wearing a ring," he stated.

She understood it to be a question. "No. No ring."

"And you said Annie has been checking for bulletins about your disappearance and hasn't found any."

"Right."

"If you had a husband," he reasoned in a tight, level voice, "he would report your disappearance. And you'd be wearing his ring." His jaw hardened. "You're not married."

"Probably not."

Neither had to voice the doubt that held them painfully arrested. *Probably* not.

He sat for a long moment clenching his jaw and staring at her. He then swore softly, set his wineglass aside and turned toward the fire, where he stared for a while longer. "Are you sure you don't remember anyone, Sarah?"

"No one at all."

He slanted her an oddly doubtful glance. "Not even...Jack?"

"Jack?"

"You said the name in your sleep."

"I did? I said 'Jack'?" She set her wineglass on the hearth to keep from spilling it as her pulse skipped and raced. A clue, at last! A clue that might open the door to memories! "Jack," she repeated, searching her mind hopefully for a glimmer of recognition.

None came.

"How did I say it?" she asked, frustrated at her inability to remember. "Did I sound scared, or...or...relieved, or..."

"You just said it." He looked rather sullen. "You'd been moaning and sobbing a little, and then you whispered, 'Jack.'"

She tried again to put a face to the name. "I don't remember him." Her lips compressed in disappointment. "If I dreamed about him, why can't I remember him?"

Connor blew out a harsh breath that could have passed for a laugh. "Here you are, racking your brain to remember—" his mouth slanted in self-deprecation "—and I'm half hoping you won't. I know it's crazy, and selfish of me—" his voice grew soft and hoarse "—but whoever this Jack is, I don't want him in the picture."

Her heart thudded and she lost herself in the heat of his tumultuous stare.

"I want you, Sarah," he said in a gruff, drawn-out whisper. "Damn it all to hell...I want you."

She wanted him, too.

Connor read it in her eyes and, before reason could stop him, he kissed her. Her lips opened for him, sweet and lush...the taste he'd been craving since their last kiss. This one quickly grew hot, probing and sexual.

He molded her body to his, from breast to thigh, but still, he needed more of her. His hands surged around every curve, filling themselves with her exquisite softness.

She moaned and moved against him in ways that provoked him to a maddening hardness. He'd never wanted with such urgency; never kissed with such compelling need.

He found her breasts beneath the chambray shirt, imprisoned by the stretchy swimsuit. Impatiently he pushed it down, out of his way, and filled his hands with warm, silky perfection.

Her mouth broke from his and she gasped his name as her nipples hardened into points against his kneading palms. He kissed her jaw, then swirled his tongue in savoring laps down the length of her throat. He wanted to fill his mouth with her....

"Connor," she cried, catching at his shoulders. "Wait."

He paused, his lips against her velvet skin, his heart pounding. They'd need protection, he realized. She would tell him they needed protection. He'd find some....

"We can't do this," she whispered.

He raised his head to meet her gaze, to assure

her that they could. The look in her eyes stopped him. Beside the undeniable longing, he saw regret.

Regret.

"I might be married."

Something painful lurched in his chest. "You're not."

"We don't know if I am."

"Then you're not."

Blinking back moisture that sprang to her eyes, she pressed a brief kiss to his cheek. Never had a kiss disturbed him more. "I have to find out," she said.

He shut his eyes and leaned his forehead against hers. He couldn't, wouldn't, let her go.

Her hands settled over his, which still cradled her breasts beneath the shirt. "I'm sorry," she whispered. "I shouldn't have kissed you back."

Drawing in a much-needed breath, he slowly released her. With a gaze meant to hammer the point home, he uttered, "Don't *ever* not kiss me back."

Rising to his feet, he felt as shaken as if he'd stuck a wire into a light socket. He shoved his hand through his sweat-dampened hair and paced across the empty room to stare blindly out into darkness through the front bay window.

Reason came back to him in slow, painful increments. As much as he hated to face it, she'd been right to stop him. She could be a married woman. Another man's wife. And she might still be in love with him—her husband, the one she couldn't remember. They might have children together. A family.

The ultimate complication.

He wanted to break something, to smash his fist through a wall and scream and rant.

And make love to her anyway.

What the hell was happening to him? He had his life laid out neatly before him, exactly as he'd wanted it. Contentment, professional success, kinship within his community. He had no need for Sarah Flowers, if that was even her name. He had no need for her.

Except that he did.

He turned back to her and found that she'd risen, smoothed her billowing hair into a silky mass of waves around her shoulders, and now waited near the door. His heart stood still. She was ready to leave.

"If you want to take me to the hotel now, I'll understand."

"If you think I want to take you anywhere other than the next room," he replied hoarsely, "you don't understand at all." He paced toward her, wanting her back in his arms. "How long do you think your money would last if you stay at a hotel?"

"Not long," she admitted. "Would you consider making me a loan? I'll pay it all back, with interest. It might take me a while, but—"

"You can have all the money you need," he promised, stopping a short distance away from her, "but I don't want you staying at a hotel." He anchored an arm against the log wall, very near to where she stood. "Stay here, Sarah. You can have my guest bedroom."

"I can't stay in town if I don't have a job, and when word gets around about Lorna firing me—

and her reasons for it—I doubt if anyone will hire me. I couldn't blame them. A lot of people saw us leave the pool together. I have no work history or references to prove my reliability. I don't even have a social security number."

He understood now why she'd valued her job with Lorna so much. And he realized how impossible it would be for her to find another one in Sugar Falls. By tomorrow, the people who could afford to hire her would close ranks against her. He'd had those ranks closed against him when he was a boy...and only because of his unconventional upbringing. Chances were slim of doors opening for a woman accused of wrongdoing.

"I know someone who could use a housekeeper," he said.

"You do?"

"Me."

"You don't need a housekeeper."

"Look around. I've got boxes and furniture stacked ceiling-high in both spare bedrooms. I moved in three months ago and haven't had time to unpack. My practice keeps me busy." Not quite the truth. He could have found the time. He simply hadn't seen the need to unpack more than he would use. He saw the need now—to keep her here. "I don't cook much. I live on cold cuts and fast food. That's enough to kill anyone. You'd be saving my life by cooking for me."

"Do you really want me to stay," she asked with hesitant hope, "as your housekeeper?"

"Yes." He wanted her as much more than that.

As their gazes melded and shifted, she whispered, "Do you think it would be wise?"

"No."

She flushed and glanced away. He could almost read her thoughts as she reviewed her alternatives.

He disrupted the process by turning her face toward his. "I'd never pressure you into anything," he swore, his fingers lingering at her jawline. "I can't say that I don't want you, or that I won't think of kissing you whenever you're near me, but—"

"And I can't say I'll always be levelheaded enough to stop you."

He drew in a breath, fighting the urge to kiss her now. He had to keep his head. He couldn't take advantage of her vulnerability. He released a frustrated sigh. "We have to find out who you are, Sarah. We can't just wait and hope that you'll remember."

"I have a plan that might jog a few memories."

"What plan?"

"I thought I'd go to Denver, to the scene of the accident, and walk around the neighborhood. See if I remember anything."

"I'll drive you there, whenever you're ready. And if you don't remember anything substantial, I'll hire a private detective. *If* you approve."

"A private detective? That would cost a fortune."

"I'll pay for it."

"Oh, Connor." She caught his face between her hands. "You're doing too much for me already. I feel guilty enough as it is. Kissing you, then pushing you away. Accepting the job you offered, but—"

"You're accepting it?"

Self-consciously, as if she'd just realized that

she'd touched him, she lowered her hands from his face. "I suppose I am."

He smiled. So did she.

Though he knew he shouldn't, he drew her to him in a celebratory hug. She didn't seem to mind. "I'll get your suitcase from the car," he whispered, keenly relishing the scent of her hair and the feel of her in his embrace. "You can stay in the guest bedroom. There's not much other than a bed set up in it, and a lot of unpacked boxes."

"It'll be perfect. Thank you, Connor...for everything you're doing for me."

"There's something else I can do," he said. "As a doctor."

She cocked a questioning glance at him.

"You asked my nurse at the office whether I could tell if you've ever had a baby." He gently brushed a silky tendril from her eyes. "I could, Sarah. I could tell you. Tonight."

6

SHE SPENT AN ENTIRE HOUR showering, soothing herself with fragrant skin lotion, leisurely drying her hair and dressing for the night. When she had finished, she still hadn't decided what that night would hold.

He'd offered her a quick, simple exam that could tell her, here and now, whether she'd ever given birth. She could know whether she was someone's mother…someone who might be waiting for her, crying for her, wondering where she'd gone. The possibility tore at her heart.

If she'd had a baby, she'd go to the authorities immediately about her amnesia, despite the fear that pounded through her at the very thought. She couldn't abandon her children.

She could know tonight, from one simple exam.

She'd told Connor she'd think about it. Over the past hour, she'd thought about nothing else, vacillating wildly between *yes* and *no*. She desperately wanted the information the exam could give her—she didn't want to wait even another day—but she couldn't quite come to grips with the idea of allowing him, Connor, to perform that exam.

Her long, silky nightgown and matching robe—a gift from Annie while she'd been in the hospital—wafted around her in the cool shadows of the log home as she approached the living room. Her heart thudded in her throat.

He sat in the leather recliner wearing the faded jeans he'd put on earlier and a soft white shirt left open, allowing a shadowed glimpse of his muscled, furred chest. His short-cropped hair and tanned skin shimmered bronze in the firelight. He looked strong, handsome and intensely virile, his elbow anchored on the armrest, his jaw resting against his fist as he stared at the fire.

There was nothing doctorly about him now.

The flames hissed, crackled and sent shadows dancing across the log walls and high-beamed ceiling. The smoky scent of kindling and oak mixed with the fragrance of the wine they'd left unfinished on the hearth. The mountain night pressed close around the log home, cloaking them in intimate seclusion.

He glanced up at her before she'd said a word. His vivid hazel eyes made a slow sweep over her face, her unbound hair, her peach-colored nightgown and her satin slippers as she stood near his bedroom doorway.

His gaze returned to hers with an added warmth. He gestured to an armchair that had somehow appeared beside his recliner since she'd left.

The silk of her nightgown billowed and whispered against her skin as she crossed the room and settled into the armchair. She couldn't help but notice how close he'd set the chair to his—close, and at an intimate angle for a heart-to-heart chat.

"Well?" he said.

She knew what he was asking, but she hadn't

quite reached a decision. The virile sensuality that clung to him like a fragrance was quickly tipping the scales against anything remotely clinical.

"As much as I'd like to know whatever information you could tell me," she began with a nervous catch in her voice, "I don't believe I can accept your...your kind offer."

He shifted forward, bringing the recliner to a fully upright position and his bare feet solidly to the floor. Resting his muscled forearms across his thighs, he leaned closer to her, his gaze disconcertingly direct. "Why not?"

Warmth flooded her face. His nearness made it harder to put her reticence into words. "I'd be too embarrassed."

He didn't reply. He simply maintained a steady watch on her eyes, her lips, her expression, as if waiting for a revealing glimpse of the reasons she withheld from him.

"I know you're a doctor, and I'm sure you're a good one," she babbled, looking everywhere but at him, "and you've probably performed examinations on millions of women...."

"Maybe not millions."

"Whatever. I feel our relationship is too personal. And an exam would be too clinical."

"The exam would involve little more than a glance, Sarah."

"A glance?" She swallowed hard and risked a peek at him. "A glance at what?"

"Various areas of the body. First I'd check for obvious signs, like a scar from a cesarean section, or—"

"There's nothing like that. Or stretch marks, or anything. I've looked."

"Then the next place I'd check is the perineum."

She wasn't sure exactly what he meant, but, of course, she had a vague idea of the general vicinity.

Gently he explained, "Where babies make their entrance into the world."

Her embarrassment intensified, but she whispered, "And you would know if one had?"

"Pretty definitely."

She stared at him in agonizing indecision. "No," she finally proclaimed. "I can't go through with it. I'm sure you don't understand, but—"

"Actually, I do. You feel uneasy because we'd be skipping ahead in the natural progression that develops between a man and a woman." A familiar gruffness softened his voice. "That's what we are to one another, Sarah. Man and woman, not doctor and patient. And you know what else?" He leaned in closer, as if to tell her a secret. "That's the way I want it."

The sheer sensual force of his gaze kept her mesmerized, and breathless, and helplessly responsive.

"When I look at you," he said, "I don't see a specimen of human anatomy and all its parts. I see you, the woman I want. There's nothing clinical about it. It's personal," he whispered. "Very, very personal." His gaze settled on her mouth, and he swept his thumb lightly across it, sending tiny shock-waves through her. "When I look at you, Sarah, or touch you, I get turned on. I won't pretend otherwise."

Her eyelids dipped at the rush of sensuality that

pooled warm and low within her. How could she think when he distracted her so with his stirring whispers and touches?

"Are you agreeing with me, then," she asked in a haze of disarming warmth, "that we shouldn't go through with the exam?"

He slid his hands along the outside of her thighs to her hips and pulled her forward in the chair, until her knees were imprisoned by his. "I'm saying," he whispered, his mouth very near hers, "that we should keep it personal. Come to bed with me, Sarah. Let me hold you, and touch you, and do whatever comes naturally. And somewhere along the way, in the natural progression of things, you won't be embarrassed at anything we do...or at any way I look at you."

Her pulse leaped, and she wanted badly to do what he was suggesting. But it hadn't been easy to stop him when they'd been kissing, and she didn't want to lead him on again. "Doesn't that 'natural progression' lead to lovemaking?"

"It doesn't have to."

"Until I know I'm not married, it can't."

She felt his muscles clench, although his gaze and his voice remained steady. "What makes you think you're married? There's not one shred of evidence that points to it."

"There's not one shred of evidence that points to anything about my past."

"Do you feel married? Do you feel you belong to someone else?"

"No. The very idea of marriage seems alien to me. So does lovemaking. What we were doing down there on the floor—" her whisper wavered

"—the way you were kissing me, touching me, and how it made me feel..." She paused, searching for words. "I don't believe I've ever felt that kind of heat before."

His hands tightened at her hips and his chest expanded beneath his open shirt, as if he'd had to drag in a breath. "What are you afraid of, Sarah?" he implored.

"I'm afraid of falling in love with you."

Something deep and hot darkened in his eyes. "I run the same risk." The statement hovered intimately between them. "If you think we can save ourselves from that by not making love," he whispered, "then we won't make love."

The muscles of her throat constricted as she swallowed and forced herself to nod. *If only things were different.*

"We'll just...explore," he said.

"Explore?"

"We'll take our time. Get comfortable with each other. And along the way, we'll find out all we can about you."

Her heart tripped into double time.

He held out his hand to help her up.

The silence of the house roared in her ears as he led her to his bedroom, where she barely noticed the spaciousness, or the fireplace in the far corner or the masculine accents in warm autumn colors. The most dominant feature, at least to Sarah's eyes, was the neatly made, king-size bed.

He stopped beside it and turned down the Indian-print spread.

Slowly, then, he approached her. "You won't need this." She didn't contradict him as he untied the fastenings and pushed the robe off her shoulders. The silky peach fabric wafted to the floor. "And I won't need my shirt." He shrugged out of it, letting it fall beside the robe. "Or my jeans." He unsnapped them, but paused. His gaze pointedly met hers. "Will I?"

"I...I suppose not."

He unzipped the faded jeans and pushed them down his powerful legs, leaving his lean, muscular body clothed in only a pair of briefs. A wide, long swell of hardness strained against the white cotton.

"Are you sure this won't be unfair to you?" she managed to whisper, trying not to stare as heat prickled beneath her skin. "I mean...when we stop."

He approached her with a wry lift of his mouth. "If you're talking about my, uh, reaction—" he glanced downward, then slowly back up to her with hypnotic hazel eyes "—it's been a chronic problem since I met you. Don't give it another thought."

She sat down at the very edge of the bed, her knees shaky and her heartbeats erratic. She couldn't quite "not give it another thought." She found herself wanting to touch him; to feel the hardness with her hand and fingers....

"You're scared," he murmured, drawing closer.

"No. A little nervous, maybe."

He sat down on the bed beside her, the hair on his thighs and muscled arms glinting gingery in the lamplight. His natural scent, male and dangerously provocative, heightened a primal awareness within her. "Nervous at what we might find?" he queried. "Or what we might do?"

"Both." She felt her nipples hardening beneath the silk of her nightgown just from the slow, hot pull of his gaze.

"No need to be nervous, Sarah." The sound of her name in his low, rich, languorous voice touched her like an intimate caress. "The whole idea is to get comfortable with each other."

Comfortable. That didn't seem to fit her mood, or his.

"In the natural progression of things between a man and a woman," he continued in a throaty whisper, "first we'd gaze into each other's eyes." He turned her face toward his, and they stared deeply, silently. A hint of humor glistened through the sensuous warmth. "We do that quite nicely, wouldn't you say?"

An answering smile touched her mouth. "I'd say so."

"And we would talk, which we've done pretty often. You can't deny that."

"We do talk."

"And then we'd touch," he informed her softly, "in casual ways. Like...this." He took her hand and wove her fingers through his. His hand felt large, warm, protective. "Or, this." He slipped a strong arm around her shoulders and nestled her against him. Beneath his velvet-smooth flesh, she felt his muscled strength and sensed an awesome power barely held in check. Her blood hummed in helpless response. "This doesn't bother you, does it?"

She shook her head, thoroughly distracted by his strength, his scent, his intoxicating nearness.

"Then when we're feeling a little more adventurous, I'd kiss your hand, if you'd let me. Would you?"

She would.

He brought her hand up to his mouth. He kissed the back of it once, then twice. "Your skin's so soft." He brushed his mouth across her knuckles in a lingering sweep. Tingles traveled up her arm. Turning her hand, he breathed into her palm, "I've dreamed of tasting you, Sarah."

The silky hot glide of his tongue against her palm stunned her.

Closing his eyes, he moved his mouth along each of her fingers, swirling his tongue around them, then sliding down to probe the valleys. Keen sensations coursed through her and forced her lips to part in a silent cry.

When he reached her little finger, he slid it all the way into his mouth and sucked. A languorous heat began deep in her belly.

He lifted his face from her hand, and his gaze simmered with barely repressed longing. "I get a little jumbled here on what should come next," he whispered hoarsely, "but I'd say your arm, since it's so conveniently attached."

She watched in silence, her heart thudding and prancing as he kissed his way across her wrist and up her arm to its sensitive crook, where he licked and lapped and lightly bit.

She caught her breath, closed her eyes and let a soft, purring sound roll from her throat. If she'd ever felt such provocative sensations, surely nothing would have made her forget them! She felt herself tipping back against fresh-scented pillows as he mouthed a tingling path to the top of her arm.

He surprised her by licking the tender curve between her arm and breast.

She cried out at the ticklish yet erotic pleasure and squeezed her arm reflexively against her side. He'd shifted, though, and now nipped at the round crest of her shoulder. She laughed breathlessly and squirmed as he rubbed his abrasive chin on her neck.

"Say it again," he whispered against her ear, breathing into its delicate shell and nipping at its lobe.

"W-what?"

He gazed heatedly at her mouth. "Say 'Ahhh.'"

He'd said it like a sensuous sigh, and when she did the same, he slid his tongue along the inside of her lips, around the inner rim of her mouth, his head moving in a slow, circular path. With every pass he made, her sensitivity grew, until she groaned, caught his face between her hands and coaxed him in deeper.

He tangled his tongue with hers. The kiss quickly caught fire, and its heat engulfed them.

Connor's hands surged around every curve, hungry for the feel of her. He savored all he could through the interfering silk, then pushed the straps from her shoulders and the gown from her breasts. He filled his hands with creamy softness, circling her nipples with his thumbs, strumming across them until they strained in ultimate hardness.

She whimpered into his mouth and arched beneath him on the bed.

Feverishly he broke from their kiss and bent to her breasts, laving them with his tongue, sucking their rigid points, pulling at them with his lips. She cried out in groans and whimpers, clutching his back and shoulders, digging her fingers into his muscles.

Desire ripped through him. He stripped the gown off her, consuming with his eyes the beauty he uncovered. He hadn't expected perfection; hadn't needed it. But she *was* perfection, straight from a wicked fantasy—sleek, lean and incredibly lush.

He ran his hands freely over her, the fire inside him leaping as she arched and undulated beneath his long, rough, coveting caresses. He trailed his hands with his mouth, sucking in succulent tastes at the swell of her breasts, the flare of her hips, the taut curve of her abdomen.

She'd closed her eyes, he noticed. Her lips were parted. Her breasts rose and fell with her labored breathing, their pointed crests glistening from his ministrations. He'd never seen a sexier sight in his life, or one that affected him more.

With hands that trembled, he peeled the lacy edge of her panties down from her moist, hot skin and drove his tongue along a salty path above dark curls.

She gasped and groaned and undulated.

He throbbed with the need to rip her panties off, capture those maddening hips and drive himself deeply into her. The very force of that need jarred him back into awareness of what he was doing.

He was losing control. He'd forgotten about "exploring," and about the object of their mission— about everything except his raging need to have her.

But he couldn't have her. He'd promised to stop.

Shutting his eyes in an excruciating effort to rein in his desire, he pressed his face against the silk of her panties, damp and fragrant with the tangy, womanly scent of her.

Aroused all the more, he fought the urge to thrust his fingers inside, to pump them into her honeyed warmth and follow through with hard, explosive sex.

Instead, he gripped her mobile hips and pinned them to the bed. His heart thundered. His fever raged. "Sarah." He felt the sweat beading on his face as he panted and fought for control. "We have to back up. I think I skipped a few steps in the, uh, natural progression."

Tremulous panting punctuated her whisper, too. "Feels natural enough to me." He felt her heart drumming as wildly as his own.

He gritted his teeth until they hurt. He could make love to her, he knew. If he hadn't already seduced her into wanting it, he couldn't be far away. She was too responsive to resist for long; too hot and aroused.

"Doesn't the natural progression lead to lovemaking?" she'd asked. *"Until I know I'm not married, it can't."*

He softly, vividly, cursed. He hadn't set out to seduce her. He'd intended to find the information she wanted—a relatively simple matter. But somewhere along the way, another motivation had worked itself into his consciousness: to make her come, with his fingers and his mouth, again and again, until her fear came true. Until she fell in love with him.

Crazy to think that sex could make her fall in

love, but she seemed to believe it could happen. Crazy for him to want her to fall in love...but he did.

And he'd never been one to swerve from a goal he'd set for himself.

With his blood throbbing in his temples and his arousal achingly hard, he yanked her panties in purposeful tugs down the curve of her hips, past glistening curls, down long, elegant legs.

The sight and scent of her naked beneath him fired him to the very brink of reason. With an impatience he couldn't help, he slid his hands up her satiny legs, gripped the undersides of her thighs and spread them. An involuntary growl reverberated in his throat as he leaned in and indulged.

Sarah gasped at the hot, wet glide of his tongue over highly sensitive folds. The intimacy of what he was doing shocked her, and she felt she should stop him.

She really should stop him....

But his eyes were closed in such intense concentration, his virile face beaded with sweat...and the lingering licks he lavished between her legs sent seductive pleasure dancing along every nerve ending in her body. His tongue glided along intimate ridges, then lashed across them in unexpected flicks that set her to trembling.

A pleasured sob escaped her.

He growled and plunged deeper—swirling, probing, sucking with a profound intensity. She cried out and closed her eyes, lost to the sensations coursing through her like molten rivers.

He shoved her leg over his muscled shoulder for greater access, then drove his tongue into her. She bucked up off the bed in a rigid arch. He gripped her hips and relentlessly pressed on.

A tear slipped from her eye and trickled past her ear to the pillow; a keening sound issued from her throat. The sensations grew sharp and intense, building into an exquisite need...a clawing, ravenous need.

And when she thought she could take no more, his finger pushed inside her, hard and large and invasive.

Her gasp mingled with some hoarse utterance of his as a climax ripped through her body. Wave after wave of white-hot pleasure broke and frothed within her.

He kept his finger inside her as she tightened around it, trapping him in a vise-like hold between her thighs.

They remained that way for a breathless eternity before he cautiously withdrew his finger. The withdrawal itself caused quivers and shivers of reaction.

He disengaged himself from her thighs and caught her to him in a hard embrace. She trembled, panted and curled against him, stunned by the intensity he'd invoked.

"Sarah." His hoarse, tremulous whisper reverberated against her temple, sending shivers down her spine. He sounded every bit as shaken as she. He tightened his arms around her, his heart hammering. "You're a virgin."

It took a moment for the information to penetrate her post-orgasmic haze.

"A virgin," he repeated.

The concept didn't surprise her as much as it

seemed to surprise him, but the ramifications un-
folded for her in exceedingly slow motion.

"Are you sure?" she whispered, almost afraid to
believe.

"Very."

Her mind whirred with realizations.

Connor shifted her onto her back and raised
himself above her. A poignant relief clouded his
eyes and crammed his chest to overflowing.
"You're not married, Sarah. You can't be married."

"I'm not married," she acknowledged in a tone
of discovery.

"And of course, you've never had a baby.
You've never..." His throat closed up and he
forced out a harsh breath. He wanted her so badly
he wasn't sure he'd be able to breathe at all.

Gladness blossomed in her eyes and shimmered
on her lips. Because he couldn't possibly stop himself from kissing her, he pressed a carefully re-
strained kiss beside her mouth, and another on her
fine-boned jaw.

"Am I *still* a virgin?" Her skin heated beneath
his lips. "Even after what we just did?"

"Absolutely."

"But, how? I mean, wouldn't the barrier have
broken?"

He searched for a way to explain. "I didn't go in
very far." After a few thudding heartbeats, he
added, "Or...with much."

Her color deepened. "It felt like you did."

His arousal, still taut with need, pulsed to a
painful hardness and his throat went dry. "Just a
finger, and not all the way. It might have felt like

more because..." His voice grew gravelly. "Because you're so tight."

Her gaze roamed his face, then returned to his eyes with languid sensuality. "Go in with more," she whispered.

Heat rushed to his head, making him dizzy. "More?"

She slipped her hand into his hair and drew his head down. He met her in a luscious parry of erotic tongue-play. "Go all the way in," she further specified in a honeyed whisper, "with everything you've got."

He didn't wait for a more explicit invitation. He didn't pause to let her reflect. He didn't ask if she was sure.

He took her mouth in a hard, consuming kiss, burning with an emotion that thoroughly possessed him. He pushed his briefs down to his thighs, gripped her hips and levered himself slowly, forcefully—irrevocably—into her.

No matter what memories might return, no matter who had shared her past, she would now be his.

SHE WAS GONE FROM HIS BED when he woke up, which surprised and disappointed him. They'd fallen asleep holding each other last night, exhausted from their lovemaking.

He'd never known lovemaking like that. He still felt shaken and awed. His need had reached a fever pitch, and when he'd finally entered her, a torrent of emotion had transported him to a dimension beyond reason or pleasure.

Had that gut-wrenching emotional response been caused by the fact that he'd taken her virginity? He was sure that had at least something to do with it—the sharp, physical sensations of breaking through a barrier and embedding himself in hot, virgin tightness; the odd mixture of regret and reverence he'd felt at her initial start of pain; the honor and the wonder of being her first; the excruciating effort it had taken to move slowly and minimally within her; the deep, primal triumph that had built along with his climax and had rocked him just as much. He'd exploded with stunning force, unable to curb the deep thrusts and violent spasms of his release.

And as he'd held her tightly afterward, he'd felt in his heart, in his bones, that she now belonged to him.

The feeling had been factually groundless, of course. He'd taken her virginity, but in today's world, had staked no real claim on her.

Unless she'd fallen in love with him.

He shook his head at his ridiculous musings. He knew that sex alone did not produce love or guarantee a relationship. Sex, he knew, could be a double-edged sword.

Why had she left his bed?

With a glance at the clock, he realized it was only seven on a Sunday morning. Plenty of time to start their day. For now, he wanted to bring her back to bed, to show her how much better lovemaking would be for her now that she'd feel no pain. Or, at least, not as much pain. She would be sore for at least a day.

A day suddenly seemed like forever.

"Barbarian," he called himself as he climbed out of bed, belted his dark blue flannel robe and set out to find her. From the hallway outside his bedroom, he heard the shower running in the bathroom. The *guest* bathroom, not the one in his master suite.

Nothing odd about that. She'd showered and changed in the guest bathroom yesterday evening. Why should she suddenly use his, just because it was more convenient to his bedroom?

Determined to keep an optimistic outlook, he ambled into the kitchen and made coffee. In a few minutes, he heard the shower turn off. He did not, however, hear the bathroom door open, even after a long while had passed. He drank a cup of coffee, brought in the Sunday-morning newspaper, took a quick shower and shaved. Before he dressed for the day, though, he shrugged into his robe again and glanced out into the hallway to see if she'd come out of the bathroom yet.

She obviously had. The bathroom stood dark and vacant, and now the door of his guest bedroom was closed.

He knocked on the bedroom door. "Sarah, are you okay?"

"Yes, I'm fine."

"Are you sure?"

"Of course."

"Will you please open this door?"

It was a while before the door finally opened. She stood with her hand poised on the doorknob, as if she might shut it again. She was dressed in slim-fitting jeans and a wide-necked mauve T-shirt that had slipped to one side, leaving a shapely shoulder bare. Her dark hair was drawn back in a French braid that lay over the one bare, tan shoulder. A hint of apprehension shone in her wide gray eyes.

"Yes?" she said.

He leaned against the doorjamb and studied her. She looked young, innocent and remarkably beautiful, and just a glance at her filled him with a warm craving. Her distant air sent a clear signal, though. He could no sooner touch her than if they'd been strangers. God...did she regret making love?

"I, uh, made coffee," he mumbled, feeling as if he'd been sucker-punched in the stomach. "Decaf, after your caffeine overdose yesterday."

"Oh!" A delicate pink climbed into her cheeks. "Thank you, but I should have made the coffee. My first day on the job and I haven't even thought about breakfast."

"On the job." He frowned. "Sarah—"

The doorbell chimed.

They both glanced in surprise toward the front door. Before he could begin to guess who might be intruding at this early hour on a Sunday, Sarah slipped past him and scurried off into the kitchen. With his insides tying themselves in knots over the possibility that she regretted making love to him, Connor answered the door.

"Connor, good morning!"

"Mimsey." He managed not to groan. He didn't have time now to deal with the terminally perky blonde from his office. It was hard enough dodging her personal attentions there; he certainly wouldn't encourage her to visit his home. Besides, he needed to talk to Sarah.

"Ham-and-cheese quiche." She lifted up a casserole dish he hadn't noticed in her hands. "Thought you could use a good breakfast after the rough time you must have had last night, poor dear." Pursing her crimson lips into an artfully sympathetic pout, she thrust the warm glass dish into his hands and stepped in the door.

He stared blankly at her. *Rough time last night?*

She cast a provocative glance at his chest, partially visible beneath the bathrobe, then down to his bare calves and feet. "I hope I didn't wake you, Connor." A dimple flashed in her cheek and her doll-blue eyes glinted. "Lorna told me this morning that you had some medical emergency to handle last night. I was *so-o-o* concerned when you two didn't show up at the dance. I know she was terribly disappointed, but I, of course, understand the demands of a doctor's job." She edged past him into the living room. "Was it one of our regular patients?"

"Uh, no."

She vampishly raked a long section of her blond hair back from her face with squared crimson nails and arched a brow in curiosity. "Nothing serious, I hope?"

"Mimsey..." He handed the casserole back to her. "I appreciate your thoughtfulness, but I've already had breakfast, and I don't—"

"We'll have it for lunch, then." With a slight roll of her bare shoulders, her breasts jutted into prominence beneath a thin, flowered halter top. She was wearing the tightest, shortest shorts he'd ever seen. "I'll just go put it in the refrigerator for later."

"I'd rather you leave, Mimsey. I have a lot to do today."

"But it's Sunday. You have to take at least one day off for—" She stopped and stared in the direction of the fireplace.

He followed her stare to the two half-full wineglasses he'd left on the hearth last night...and to Sarah's handbag and sandals a short distance away.

A ruddy flush rose beneath Mimsey's perfect tan. Slowly she turned to him with a perfunctory smile. "Since you're so...busy, I guess I'll be on my way. You probably need to rest after your 'emergency' last night."

He pursed his lips to stifle an unwise grin as he handed her back the quiche.

This time, she took it.

As CONNOR ENTERTAINED in the living room, Sarah cracked an egg into a bowl of biscuit batter and beat it fiercely with a wooden spoon. From the one quick peek she'd taken at Connor and his blond visitor, she knew that Mimsey had brought him breakfast.

Which meant she didn't have to make the biscuits. She had to keep busy, though, or she'd feel like a fool. Mimsey might be staying to share that quiche with Connor.

She almost whipped the batter right out of the bowl.

This wouldn't do. This simply wouldn't do. She couldn't afford to care so much.

The lovemaking—the feverish, exhilarating lovemaking—had been a mistake. She'd known it when she'd opened her eyes this morning and found herself curved intimately against his naked body, his arm wrapped around her and his hand cradling her breast as he slept. She'd wanted to stay that way forever, tucked safely in his arms, skin to skin, wonderfully sated from a night of lovemaking. Moments later, she'd wanted more than that. She'd wanted to wake him with kisses and start their lovemaking all over again.

But then she'd gazed into his sleeping face and felt such an overwhelming tenderness that she could scarcely breathe.

She could so easily fall in love with him.

She couldn't allow that! The fear that brewed within the fog of her lost memories touched her again in grim warning. She would bring him harm—grave bodily harm. She wasn't sure how, where, or when, but she knew it would happen. She'd have to leave him before it did.

And she couldn't even tell him about her fear for his safety because then he'd never let her go without interfering. His protective instincts would kick into high gear and he'd become even more deeply involved in her problems.

But what if the danger isn't real? an inner voice asked. Maybe the fear was a symptom of the head trauma. As much as she wished she could believe that, she didn't.

Stop, she commanded herself, retrieving a baking pan from a cabinet. Even without the nameless danger that stalked her, having a sexual relationship with Connor would cause far too many complications. She'd spent all morning musing over them.

Realizing that the murmur of voices from the other room had stopped, she glanced toward the doorway and nearly dropped the pan.

Connor stood leaning against the kitchen counter, his hands deep in the pockets of his robe, his solemn, hazel-eyed gaze fixed on her.

"I'm making biscuits to go with the quiche," she managed to say.

"There's no quiche. Mimsey's gone."

Sarah forced her attention back to her baking. The relief she felt only emphasized how emotionally involved she already was. As she dropped dollops of batter onto the pan from a spoon, she asked without looking at him, "Would you like sausage to go with the—"

"Sarah," he interrupted, his voice gruff and quiet, "do you regret last night?"

She felt her heart rising into her throat. How could she truthfully answer that? She would treasure last night forever...and yet, she regretted it deeply. "No, no, of course I don't," she lied, turning to him with a smile meant to reassure. The smile wavered under the pressure of his stare.

"Should I have stopped?"

"Don't be silly! I asked you to keep on. I practically begged you." More reassuring words clogged in her throat, and she swallowed hard to dislodge them. "Even if I did regret it, I certainly can't blame you."

He shut his eyes, and slowly reopened them. "So then you do feel there's cause for blame."

"Oh, Connor, I didn't mean it that way." She set the spoon down and ventured a step closer to him, wishing she could distract him from this line of questioning. He didn't deserve to feel guilty, or to believe he hadn't pleased her. "Last night was wonderful, incredibly wonderful. Surely you had to know that I...I liked it."

Unreadable emotion flickered in his eyes. "But?"

She forced a smile and a lighthearted shrug. "But nothing. You told me some extremely important information about myself, which I'll always be grateful for. And of course, I also had a great time."

"A great time," he repeated. His sober, steady gaze pressed past her smile in search of a deeper truth. "Then come here," he whispered, "and kiss me."

Her smile slowly faded until she stood staring at him in pained dismay. A kiss would be too dangerous to her heart.

He caught her hands and pulled her to him as he

sat at the edge of a stool near the breakfast bar. "Tell me what's wrong, Sarah." His gaze delved into hers as he slipped an arm around her waist to stop her from escaping.

"Making love to you has complicated things," she whispered, unable to resist the draw of his gaze and the warm strength of his arm around her.

"What things?"

"My role here, for one. I've agreed to work as your housekeeper, and you've agreed to provide room and board." She paused, trying to arrange her scattered thoughts into a coherent explanation. "It wouldn't be fair to either of us to expect anything beyond that."

His brows knit together. "Are you concerned that I'm going to expect you to sleep with me as part of the job?"

She blushed, hating for him to think she was accusing him of something so low. "Not as part of the job! But sexual involvement does complicate an employer-employee relationship, especially in a situation where we'd be living together. For instance, what happened just now with Mimsey," she pointed out. "You didn't have to make her leave, but I understand why you did. She wouldn't have felt comfortable with me here, especially if she knew there was anything more between us than a working relationship."

"I didn't want Mimsey to stay, and our relationship is none of her business."

Sarah couldn't help feeling relieved, which only added to her dismay. "Maybe you didn't want her to stay right now," she argued, "but sometime you might. Would you feel comfortable bringing her, or anyone, to your house while I'm here?"

"A woman, you mean?"

"Yes, a woman. You're a single man. You have the right to bring a date home with you."

"Are you telling me that wouldn't bother you?"

It would break her heart, she realized with sudden clarity. The realization frightened her. She couldn't expect his exclusive attention. She didn't intend to deserve it.

"As your housekeeper," she said, fighting to keep her voice steady and reasonable when her throat kept wanting to close up, "I'd have no right to an opinion on the subject. I want to be fair to you, Connor. I don't want to intrude on your private life."

"Would it make you feel better if I swore to bring another woman home once a week, or maybe twice? Heck, why stop at one woman? I grew up around people who believed in free love and open relationships and even multiple partners. Is that what you're saying you want?"

"No!" She felt shaken, appalled and very near tears.

"Good. Because I don't want you to feel okay with my bringing other women home. And I sure as hell wouldn't be okay with you having other men. I'm not open-minded about these things, Sarah. I don't take sexual involvement lightly, and since you were a virgin until last night, I doubt that you do, either."

"I don't," she whispered. "And that's the problem. While I'm living here, sexual involvement with you only blurs the lines of what I can reasonably expect. It complicates things."

"Things were complicated from the first moment I met you."

The heat of his words and gaze kindled a familiar warmth within her. She couldn't succumb to this warmth. She couldn't allow her concerns to melt away in his fire—especially not the concern she hid from him.

"It's like what you were telling me last night," she said, desperate now to convince him. "In the natural progression of things between a man and a woman, I would have gone home to my own place this morning, and you'd carry on with your own life. If you felt like calling me for another date, you would. If I felt like accepting, I would. But as it is, I'm living here with you. It's too big a departure from the natural order."

He lodged her firmly, possessively, against him. "Feels natural enough to me."

Her breath caught. In her heart, she had to agree....

"Sarah." He slipped his fingers into her hair and tilted her face to his. "I don't want anyone but you," he declared in a fervent whisper. "If you don't want to sleep with me, you know you don't have to. I'll find a way to deal with it. But please—" he closed his eyes and brushed his parted lips across her mouth in frustrated longing "—please don't hold yourself apart from me."

She couldn't ignore his whispered plea. She gave in to a hot, yearning kiss. He tasted like coffee and minty toothpaste; he smelled like sandalwood; he felt like heat, hard muscle and heaven.

Heaven. He could take her there, she knew.

She wanted him to.

With a gasp, she broke away from his kiss, her pulse thrumming and her temperature soaring. She couldn't trust herself with him! One kiss and she already wanted more. "If you don't want me to keep my distance from you," she cried, "then you can't kiss me like that."

He stared at her in charged silence, his color high and his breathing hard. His jaw slowly squared. "Okay. I won't kiss you," he agreed. A disturbing sparkle entered his gaze, though, and he added, "Like that."

With a flutter of her heart, she turned away from him and slid the biscuit pan into the oven, determined to ignore the chaotic reactions he provoked within her.

"I'll go get dressed," he murmured, watching her as she adjusted the oven temperature. "And after breakfast, we'll explore."

"Explore." Her gaze whipped back to his in alarm. The word evoked a warm rush of provocative memories from the night before.

He seemed to read every one of them in her eyes. "The mountainside in my backyard," he clarified softly, "and the wooded trails along the river." The hint of a smile kicked up one corner of his mouth. "I'm sure I can take you to a few places you haven't been before."

The huskiness in his voice brought to mind all kinds of ways to circumvent the natural progression of things.

DRESSED FOR RIDING IN HIS light denim shirt, jeans, boots and Stetson, Connor escorted Sarah across the wooded, grassy backyard to his stable.

She obligingly wore her hiking boots and a riding cap he kept on hand for his guests. She'd tucked her mauve, wide-necked T-shirt into the narrow waistband of her jeans—dark, slim-fitting jeans that hugged the curves of her long legs and nicely rounded bottom in a way that made him want to touch.

Forcing his attention away from that particular temptation, he asked distractedly, "Do you ride?"

"Well, I...really don't know."

He could have kicked himself at the look of mild distress in the glance she tossed him. Of course she wouldn't know. She'd told him she didn't remember anything about her past, and even if she had once ridden, the amnesia could have erased whatever knowledge she'd had. A tricky thing, amnesia. There was no accounting for what was forgotten and what was retained.

"You can ride with me," he told her as they approached his stable. "Or if you'd prefer, we can explore the lake and river by boat. Which sounds better? Horse or boat?"

"They're both new to me."

He swung open the stable door and ushered her inside. The smell of horse and hay greeted them, and her first reaction wasn't all that promising. She halted just inside the stable door and peered wordlessly at his two horses in their stalls.

"This is Wind Dancer," he told her, patting his roan colored mare affectionately on the neck. "And the stallion is Viking, the one we'll ride today."

She didn't reply or make any move whatsoever, and he wondered if she was afraid.

"You can have a seat on that stool over there while I get him ready." He strolled toward the stallion's stall. "Since we'll be riding double, the most comfortable way would be bareback."

She murmured something he didn't quite catch, and when he glanced back at her, he did a double take.

She stood beside Wind Dancer, rubbing the mare's neck and gently scratching between her eyes. "You're a sweet girl, Wind Dancer," she murmured. "And you like to be scratched, don't you?"

Surprise and gladness kept him speechless. She wasn't afraid of horses, and judging from the look of sheer contentment in Wind Dancer's eyes, Sarah knew how to win their hearts.

His next surprise came after he'd led Viking out of the stable, bridled but without a saddle. "You ready to give this a try?" he asked Sarah.

Her eyes sparkled with pleasurable anticipation. "Okay."

Before he had the chance to help her mount, she took hold of Viking's mane, swung her right leg over his rump and settled lightly onto his back.

Connor stared at her in dazed admiration. That wasn't a mount that any novice would have tried, and she'd accomplished it with a graceful ease that many experienced riders would envy.

"Are you getting on, or not?" she asked, gathering the reins in her hands.

"Yes, ma'am." With a smile on his lips and a song in his heart, he swung up behind her.

His denim-clad thighs molded to hers, and the

nicely rounded backside he'd been noticing all morning fit snugly against his groin. Heaven, he thought, couldn't be much finer than this.

Their bodies leaned and shifted in synchrony as they rode over mountain trails and across grassy fields, reveled in the mild sunshine, springtime breeze and heady fragrance of wildflowers. She laughed aloud in pleasure, turning to share an exuberant smile with him every now and then, or to exclaim over a particularly beautiful view.

He had a hard time concentrating on the view, though. He was too distracted by the vivid, heart-stopping beauty of the woman in his arms and the feel of her against him. She warmed his heart with a rare magic, yet provoked a need in him that grew into a physical ache.

The natural movement of her body as she guided the horse intensified Connor's awareness of their intimate physical position. Just as he wondered if she could feel his arousal against her backside, he felt her body stiffen, and she cried out, "Stop, stop. Whoa, Viking! Whoa!"

The horse came to a halt beneath a huge oak tree near the river and Connor quickly dismounted, anticipating problems ranging from physical ailments to recriminations against his lusting after her.

But as he turned to help her down from the horse, she slid into his arms with a joyous smile. "I remember, Connor! I remember!"

He didn't get a word out, she hugged him so tightly.

"I had a horse of my own!" She let him go and danced away, her eyes sparkling with happiness.

"Her name was Hurricane. A white quarter horse."

"That's wonderful, Sarah."

"I remember riding her across fields, and jumping, and...and... Oh, Connor, I used to ride along a beach."

"A beach? Do you remember where?"

"Where?" She looked surprised at the question, then stared off over the river. "I don't know. There were palm trees, though, mixed in with pines and oaks."

"Palm trees. That could be California, or Florida, or...hell...almost anywhere along the gulf coast."

"And I remember a man."

"A man?" He stiffened. He wasn't sure he wanted to hear this. She'd been a virgin, but she could have been in love....

"An old stable hand. Tom, I think I called him. He used to help groom Hurricane. I can remember him so clearly, Connor, but not his last name."

Slowly he released the breath he'd been holding. "Do you remember anything else?"

She frowned in concentration, but soon shook her head. "No."

He pulled her to him. He needed to hug her, to hold her. For a terrible moment, he'd feared the worst—that she'd remember a man she'd been in love with. He couldn't take much more of the uncertainty, and he didn't believe she could, either. "Sarah, we've got to do all we can to find out about your past."

"I know." She smiled up at him. "At least the memories have started to come back." She eased away from his embrace and sat down on a boulder.

"It's funny how I can remember emotions and re-actions to people and events, but not objective de-tails. Like this morning, when I was thinking about my…" A faint blush rose in her cheeks. "My vir-ginity."

"Yeah?" he prodded when she paused, anxious to hear her feelings about the subject.

"I couldn't remember specific times, places or people, but I remember that the older I got, the more conscious I became of the fact that I was a vir-gin, and the more hesitant I became to make The Big Change. It seemed to take on so much impor-tance." She met his eyes in a search for understand-ing. "I didn't want the first time to be with just any-body."

A taut stillness came over him. "And…was it?"

"Oh, no." Unmistakable tenderness lit her gaze and softened her mouth. "Far from it."

His love for her swelled almost painfully within his chest. He couldn't allow himself to read too much into that tender gaze. He couldn't confuse fondness, physical attraction, or maybe even grati-tude for love. She'd told him, after all, that she wouldn't make love to him again, and that he couldn't even kiss her.

He'd try his damnedest to change her mind. Set-tling his hand at her delicate nape, he savored the silkiness of her skin and her dark, shining hair. "You know, making love will be better for you next time. You won't feel the pain."

"The pain was worth it," she whispered, "and I don't see how the lovemaking could get much bet-ter."

His blood heated and he leaned in for a kiss,

craving a taste of her. She angled her head and parted her lips, but before his mouth touched hers, her lashes fluttered and she pulled back.

He clenched his teeth, wanting her.

"You said you wouldn't," she reminded him.

"I said I wouldn't kiss you like I did this morning." He managed a small smile. "But I can think of all kinds of ways to kiss you, Sarah."

Her gaze had settled on his mouth and he sensed desire simmering just beneath her resistance. But the moment she realized he was drawing close again, she looked away.

"Connor," she said, sounding a little flustered, "I don't know much about you.

"Like what?"

"Do you have family?"

"Aunts, uncles and cousins, but they live out of state."

"What about parents, or siblings?"

As always, the question put him on edge. He supposed the reaction was a throwback to his young adulthood, when he'd tried so hard to separate himself from his family in the eyes of the townspeople. It had taken a medical degree from an Ivy League school and a sizable financial gain to really fix his place among them. "My father died while I was in med school, and my mother shortly after. I didn't have any real brothers or sisters."

"Real?" she repeated, puzzled.

"I grew up with other kids who were called my brothers and sisters. But…they weren't."

"Was that in the community where people believed in free love and multiple partners?"

He winced, remembering his angry outburst.

She was too perceptive for him to make slipups like that. "I shouldn't have said that, Sarah. I guess I was trying to shock you."

"But, was it true?"

"To an extent." He didn't want to talk about the free-spirited community where he had grown up; where family lines were often blurred in favor of communal living. Some kids hadn't known who their real parents were and gravitated toward whichever adult was available as a caregiver.

His mother had been different. She'd allowed no blurred lines in her marriage or her motherhood— the one concession his father had made to her.

But Connor didn't want to think about his parents, or their way of life. "Some of our neighbors professed to believe in 'free love,'" he admitted, "but I think they were more talk than action."

"Was that here, in Sugar Falls?"

"No."

"I thought you were raised here."

"Nearby."

"You went to school here, though, didn't you?"

"High school. Before that, I was homeschooled." Determined to put an end to the conversation, he stood and paced toward Viking, who was grazing peacefully beside a tree. "But my past isn't the important thing. Yours is." He untied the horse from the tree and glanced at Sarah. "I think it's time we drive into Denver and see if you remember anything at the scene of the accident."

"Now?"

"It's only a couple hours." He glanced at his watch. "We can be there by three." Uneasiness had crept into her gaze, and he added quietly, "I'll be there with you, Sarah, every step of the way."

Oddly enough, at his assurance her uneasiness seemed to deepen into fear. She looked as if she might refuse. But after a long hesitation, she asked, "Can I stop and buy a hat and sunglasses?"

"So you won't be recognized?"

"Whoever was chasing me when I ran out into the street might still be around there...looking for me...."

"We'll do it any way you want." He wanted to rid her of that fear he saw in her eyes. "But I think we need to do it now."

Drawing in a deep, shaky breath, she nodded.

THEY RETURNED SHORTLY before midnight. The trip had been neither a total waste nor a total success. Although they'd walked the streets of Denver near the accident site and driven down countless others, Sarah hadn't remembered anything new. During their long drive, though, they'd talked. Questions he'd posed to her had brought back a few more details.

She'd told him about a party where people had been lifting glasses of wine and toasting her. She couldn't recall the occasion or the faces, but as Connor asked her about the place, she remembered she had been in her apartment. Slowly details came back to her about the furniture, wall hangings and the view of a neat, quiet city street from the balcony. Nothing gave them a clue to its whereabouts.

He'd plied her with questions about her horse, and she remembered that she'd had to sell her because she was moving out of state—to Denver—but she couldn't remember where she'd been moving *from*, or how long ago the move had taken place.

He'd asked about her virginity, and how she had managed to preserve it for so long. "You must have driven a lot of guys crazy."

"I was too shy in high school to meet many boys," she recalled. "I rarely dated. And then when I started college, I spent most of my time studying and working in a veterinarian's office to pay my way."

Her eyes had widened with excitement. "College! I went to college! And I worked part-time for a vet!" But she couldn't remember which college she'd attended, the subject she'd majored in, or the name of the veterinarian she'd worked for.

She'd remembered faces of friends, a few first names and some funny anecdotes that made her laugh.

As happy as all these memories had made her, she'd grown silent and pensive during their long, dark drive home. He'd pulled her close to him and tried to ignore the anxiety clawing at him.

She would, eventually, remember her life, or piece it together from clues. He had no doubt about that. Would she then leave him to return to that life?

He unlocked the door to his log cabin and switched on a light. It was late on a Sunday night; he'd have to get up early for work in the morning. Tension, which had been building in him all day, now slowed his steps as he headed for his room.

He wanted badly to sleep with her. To take her

to his bed and hold her in his arms, if that was all she'd allow.

She, too, had paused outside the door of the guest bedroom. "Connor, thank you for taking me all the way to Denver. I know it was a long drive, and we're home late, and you have work tomorrow."

"Thank you for letting me take you." He lodged a shoulder against the wall near her. His gaze took in the beauty of her eyes, the softness of her skin, the smoothness of her lips. "I wouldn't have wanted you to go without me."

She tilted her face to his. "I'm sorry that we ended up wasting so much time."

He caressed the curve of her jaw, his insides burning with his need to kiss her. "No time spent with you is wasted."

The warmth in her gaze changed into something deeper; something solemn and heated and searching.

"Sarah," he whispered urgently, "sleep with me. We'll just sleep together, nothing more."

She slid her arm around his neck, her fingers delving into his hair. And though he'd said he wouldn't, he kissed her.

The need, the heat, the mutual longing, combusted into instant fire. Their kisses grew ravenous. By the time they'd stumbled to his bed, they'd stripped off most of each other's clothes. They were naked, hot and clenched together when they hit the mattress.

They made love late into the night—hard and needful at first, and then slow and exquisitely tender. Sarah learned that he'd been right. The lovemaking was even better this time; her responses more intense, her pleasure beyond her experience.

By morning, she knew her fear had come true. She'd fallen in love with him.

And when she'd wakened to find herself cozy and naked in his arms, another memory from her past returned to her with startling clarity. She remembered a man slipping a ring onto her finger.

A wedding ring.

8

"YOU'RE NOT MARRIED. You were a virgin. How the hell could you have been married?"

Perched at the edge of his bed wearing only her peach silk robe, Sarah anxiously chewed her lip as she watched Connor dress for work. "I know it's not too likely, but—"

"It's damn near impossible. The wedding ring was probably just a dream."

"It seemed very real, Connor. More like a memory. A man was slipping a ring onto my finger."

"I still say it was a dream. But if it wasn't, maybe the man was a salesman trying to sell you the ring." With curt precision, he buttoned the blue collarless shirt until it stretched neatly across the broad expanse of his chest.

"A wedding band? Why would I buy my own wedding band?"

He frowned, zipped up his khaki trousers and tightened the belt at his trim waist with a violent tug. "Maybe a friend was showing you a ring he bought for someone else."

"I suppose that's possible."

He shot her an emphatic glance. "You're not married." He seemed to realize how surly he sounded, and gentled his tone as he clasped his gold watch around his wrist. "You're bound to be confused as fragments of memories come back to you. Since you're not getting the whole story at once, things will be taken out of context."

She wished she could be as sure as he was. "I remember exactly what the ring looked like and felt like on my hand."

"What about the man who put the ring on you?" He'd finished dressing and now turned to stare at her, looking freshly groomed, handsome and annoyed. "Do you remember anything about him?"

"Only his hands. Big, pale hands that pushed the ring onto the third finger of my left hand."

A pulse throbbed at Connor's temple. He looked as if he were debating with himself whether or not to broach a subject. "Could his name have been... Jack?"

Distress whispered through her. "I don't know. I haven't said the name again in my sleep, have I?" she asked doubtfully.

"Not that I'm aware of."

They regarded each other in pregnant silence.

With a harsh breath, Connor pulled her up from the bed by the shoulders and conveyed his frustration with a deep, possessive kiss. "You're not married," he declared conclusively. "You were a virgin. Case closed." Gently, then, he brushed back a wayward curl from her face. "If you belong to any man, Sarah, you belong to me."

Warmth skittered through her veins. She wanted to belong to him; to belong in his life as his only woman. Nothing could please her more. And yet, after the words had been said, they tugged at some buried memory. *You belong to me.* A shiver of unease displaced the warmth.

"I said, '*If* you belong to any man,'" Connor reminded her. "I know that you don't. You're your own woman, Sarah. I just wish I could convince you of that."

The sincerity and concern in his green-brown eyes made her love him all the more. She slipped her arms around his lean waist and hugged him, treasuring the strength of his arms as they wrapped around her, the masculine scent of his skin and aftershave, the forceful beating of his heart.

"Don't worry about me," she said. "I'm sure I'll make sense of it all before very long."

"I'm going to hire a private investigator. Today."

She drew back with a troubled frown. "That's sure to cost a lot of money. I already owe you so much."

"I'm paying for it. I want to clear up all your doubts. Solve your mysteries." He tipped her face up to his. "All the unknowns are driving me crazy, Sarah. It must be a hell of a lot worse for you."

"It would be unbearable," she admitted, "if it wasn't for one Dr. Connor Wade, the sweetest, kindest, sexiest man I've ever known."

His mouth lifted in a wry half smile. "Yeah, but at this particular time, I'm the *only* man you've ever known."

"That's entirely beside the point," she retorted, knowing that he'd exaggerated only slightly.

"No, actually, that *is* the point. It's—"

She shushed him with a tender kiss.

"Mmm." He slid his hands beneath her silken robe, around her waist and along the curve of her back, pressing her naked body to his clothed one. "Mmmmm."

Passion sparked between them and heated their kiss. She felt his arousal swell and harden beneath his trousers. She moved against him in a mindlessly sensual response.

He groaned, plunged his tongue deeper into her mouth and cupped her bottom, lifting and tilting her against him. His erection pulsed strong and hot behind the cool zipper.

"Connor," she said in a breathy whisper, "you've got to go to the office."

He pulled his hips away slightly, and she felt his hand slide down between their bodies, working at his zipper. "So I'll be late," he uttered gruffly.

A sweet, torturous ache grew within the very core of her as he unbuckled his belt and pushed his pants down his muscular thighs.

"I need you, Sarah," he rasped against her ear. "I need to be inside you."

"I want you there."

He shoved the robe off her and invaded her mouth in a hot, demanding kiss. She groaned, wove her fingers into the plush depths of his hair and kissed him with all the passion he incited.

His hands coursed downward in a greedy, groping caress until at last they curved around her bottom and lifted her. His hard, blunt fingers fanned and pressed into sensitive valleys. Shards of pleasure shot through her from every probing fingertip.

She folded her legs around his powerful thighs as their mouths mated. He angled his hips and guided hers in a sleek, precise motion. Their kisses slowed, but in no way lessened. The smooth, hard tip of him teased and probed at her entrance, forcing her into wilder gyrations.

She needed—desperately needed—deeper penetration.

With a hoarse cry, Connor lodged her against the closet door and gave it. Repeatedly.

With every thrust, he gritted his teeth in an effort to withstand the pleasure; to delay the ever-nearing climax. He plunged in farther each time, aiming for nothing short of her heart. Or maybe her soul. He needed to be there. Needed to stay there.

You're mine. No one else's. Only mine.

AT NOON ON THAT WARM but overcast Monday, Sarah made the short trek down the road from Connor's house to town, then crossed the Main Street Bridge over a waterfall and into the triangle-shaped business district of Sugar Falls.

Connor had insisted she meet him for lunch.

She hadn't been too keen on the idea. "People will have heard Lorna's version of the Juneberry Lake incident. I'm not sure I'm ready to face the music."

"We'll face it together. It'll be better that way."

She didn't follow his logic. To her way of thinking, they'd only be adding fuel to the fire.

He persuaded her to come, though, by explaining he wanted to set up an account at his bank for her—a loan, as they'd agreed—to give her access to money whenever she needed it.

"I don't have identification," she reminded him.

"No bank will let me set up an account or cash checks."

"I'll set up the account. You'll have an ATM card."

She'd liked the idea of having access to cash without having to carry much around with her. And though she didn't particularly relish the idea of publicly presenting herself in town, she did look forward to having lunch with Connor.

It seemed she couldn't get enough of his company.

As she walked past quaint, awning-shaded shops, boutiques, a candy store and a hair salon, she found herself daydreaming about him. She had to smile at that. Her life was a mess, her past and future little more than question marks, but thoughts of Connor dazzled her with the sweetest, brightest happiness.

Could she possibly have fallen in love with another man the way she had with him? If so, why had she withheld her body?

The wedding band, she decided, must have been someone else's. She hoped she would remember more about it soon. It seemed likely that she would. Memories had been seeping back to her since their horseback ride yesterday.

This morning, while she'd been unpacking boxes in Connor's third bedroom, she'd remembered that she liked to dance—the swing, the cha-cha, the tango.

She also remembered that she'd owned two little Maltese dogs named Honey and Spice. She'd left them in somebody's care while she made the move to Colorado.

Who?

She tried to remember, but only drew a blank. How frustrating! She had to keep faith that the memory would surface in its own good time, along with others.

She reached Connor's office before she'd realized it. The neat, carpeted waiting room reminded her of her first visit and the agony of filling out that medical form. What a difference Connor had made in her life since then!

Just the thought of him made her heart sing.

She stepped up to the receptionist's window in the small medical office and gave her name to a prim, middle-aged brunette whose pleasant face was dominated by thick bifocals. "Could you please let Dr. Wade know I'm here?"

Before the receptionist answered, a willowy blonde rose from a chair behind her. Sarah recognized her with a ridiculous pang of dismay.

"Hello there," Mimsey greeted, her china-blue eyes glittering with barely concealed surprise and curiosity. "Sally, isn't it?"

"Sarah."

"Sarah. I'm s-o-o-o sorry, but you've come at the wrong time. The office is closing for lunch until two. And after that, Dr. Wade is booked solid. He can't handle any walk-ins."

"He's expecting me."

She arched a blond eyebrow. "Is he? Well. Isn't he a softie? He can't resist helping anyone in distress. It's why he became a doctor, you know."

Despite her determination to remain unfazed, Sarah felt her muscles clench. She couldn't deny that Connor was helping her in a time of "distress"....

"The problem," continued Mimsey, her voice oozing cordiality, "is that some people take advantage of his kindness."

A doubt shadowed Sarah's heart. *Was* she taking advantage of his kindness?

"And worse than that," Mimsey confided, "is when the person he's helping takes it for more than it is. Charity, really." She cocked her head. "You've run into trouble lately, haven't you, Sally? Something to do with losing your job?"

Sarah refused to react. "Tell him I'm here, please."

"I've buzzed him, Ms. Flowers," interjected the brown-haired receptionist, looking embarrassed. "Come on back here through that door, hon. You can wait in his office, if you'd like."

As Sarah entered the area where Mimsey and the receptionist sat behind the billing counter, Connor walked in through an opposite doorway with his nurse Gladys, quietly talking to her as he wrote out a prescription.

With his crisp, white lab coat worn casually over his shirt and khaki trousers, a stethoscope around his neck and a patient's chart in his hands, he reminded her forcibly of the first time she'd ever seen him. Her heart stood still, just as it had then. Tall, muscular, tanned and potently masculine in his doctor's garb, he had to be the sexiest man she'd ever seen.

He ripped off a page from the prescription pad, handed it along with the patient's chart to Gladys and raised his vivid hazel gaze to Sarah.

For a moment, neither of them said a word. Less than five hours had passed since they'd made passionate love against his closet door. The memory of it charged the air between them.

His gaze left hers to meander down the length of her. She'd taken time to dress for their lunch date. Leisurely he surveyed her short, casual dress, strappy high-heeled sandals and bare, tanned legs. "Hello." The male appreciation in his drawl made the word more a compliment than a greeting.

"Hello."

"You're late." A smile played in his eyes as he consulted his watch. "By two minutes and fifteen seconds."

The sunshine returned to her heart to melt away the hesitation Mimsey's words had caused. "I ran into a slight delay."

"Yeah, a cat," muttered the receptionist, glancing sideways at Mimsey. "With claws."

Connor raised his brows in question.

Sarah felt her face grow warm. She preferred to forget the humiliating insinuations Mimsey had made. "Ready for lunch?"

"Sarah, have you met everyone?" Ignoring her question, he took her arm and turned her toward Mimsey and the receptionist. "This is Joan Phelps, receptionist extraordinaire, and Mimsey Whittenhurst, whom you may have met at Lorna's. Ladies, I'd like you to meet Sarah. When she comes in, take good care of her." He slipped his arm around her waist and gazed at her with the unmistakable warmth of an intimate relationship. "I'm hoping she'll drop by for lunch on a regular basis."

With her face still uncomfortably warm—more

in response to his nearness and touch than in embarrassment—Sarah murmured polite responses to the women's greetings. Mimsey, she noticed, uttered a brief, dry reply without meeting her eyes, then busied herself with paperwork.

Connor's perceptive gaze seemed to pick up on something amiss in Mimsey's reaction. "Wait for me outside by my car, Sarah. It's parked in the side lot. I'll be there in a minute."

He waited until the door had closed behind her before addressing his two-member clerical staff. "Just in case there's any doubt, I'd like to make my feelings understood." Though he spoke to both women, his gaze remained on Mimsey. "Whenever Sarah calls or comes in, you tell me. Immediately. I don't care if I'm performing open-heart surgery on the Pope. You tell me."

"Yes, Doctor," Joan replied, casting another reproving glance at her co-worker.

Mimsey pursed her lips. "I hope you know what you're getting into, Connor. Have you taken a good look at her chart? The phone number for her previous doctor isn't valid. The area code isn't even right for the city. She's got no address or phone number, and—"

"What were you doing with her chart, Mimsey?"

"I...I was entering insurance information into the computer."

"She paid with cash."

"Cash? Yes...well...somehow her chart got mixed up in my insurance pile, and before I realized it, I'd—"

"Her chart has been in my desk drawer since her visit. At least, that's where I put it."

Mimsey stared at him, red-faced. "I'm only trying to watch out for you, Connor."

"Uh, Joan, would you excuse us for a moment, please? I'd like to talk to Mimsey in private." With a nod, Joan hurried into the back offices. Turning to Mimsey, Connor said, "The confidentiality of my patients has to come before any personal concern. You've stepped over the line, Mimsey." Holding his anger in check, he told her softly, "You're fired." Flicking on the intercom, he said, "Joan, Mimsey will be leaving us. Please help her clear out her things."

When Joan returned, Connor murmured a few discreet instructions to her, then headed for the door. With a sudden thought, he looked back at the stunned, openmouthed blonde. "Oh, and Mimsey...if anything you've learned in this office gets around town, you'll answer to my attorney."

He strode out of the office and around the corner to the side parking lot, wondering what Mimsey had said to Sarah. He wouldn't tolerate slights against her. He'd do battle with the whole damn town if he had to.

The sight of Sarah leaning against his Jaguar with a welcoming warmth in her gray eyes distracted him from his anger. The light knit of her dress—a soft shade of coral—clung to her curves in all the right places and ended mid-thigh. The short sleeves just capped her shoulders, leaving her arms provocatively bare. She'd caught her dark hair up in a twist with tendrils trailing seductively down her slender neck. And the high-heeled sandals added a wicked glamour to her long, tanned legs.

She was enough to bring any man to his knees. He was ready to drop to his now...and kiss his way up those endless legs, beneath the flirty dress, and lose himself in the taste of her. He wanted to light fires inside her so she'd wrap those legs around him again, like she had this morning....

He hooked a hand around her narrow waist and rasped into her ear, "Don't take that dress off till I get home."

A smile curved her mouth and a familiar sensuality darkened her eyes. He kissed her, forcing himself to keep it quick and light. If he didn't, he'd end up driving her home and spending his lunch hour making love to her.

Not a bad idea....

But he'd promised to take her to lunch and to the bank. Besides, he wanted the town to see them together—to know she wasn't alone; that he'd stand beside her; that whatever had happened between them on Saturday had been more than just a meaningless rendezvous at Juneberry Lake.

He wanted them to know she was his, even if she herself didn't understand that yet.

He laced his fingers through hers and pulled her into step beside him. They dodged cars as they walked across the street, then sauntered hand in hand to an outdoor café. He introduced her to the hostess who seated them, and to the owner of the café, and to an elderly couple at a table as they passed by it.

He then guided her to a cozy corner, where they ordered sandwiches. She told him about the memories that had returned that morning. He teased her into promising to teach him the tango.

She wondered aloud if her dogs, Honey and Spice, were okay. He assured her she wouldn't have left them with someone irresponsible.

"That reminds me," she said. "I'd like to check with the pound and see if Lorna really did give Tofu away."

Connor narrowed his eyes. "And if she did?"

"He'll be miserable there, Connor. And who knows if he'll find another home. He's a smart, dominant little Shih Tzu, and if he's allowed to exert that dominance, he's a joy."

"Something tells me," he said with droll dryness, "that I'm going to have a Shih Tzu living at my house who's named after soybean curd."

She beamed at him. "Really, Connor? You wouldn't mind? Timmy and Jeffrey could see him, then."

"Good Lord. I'm going to have the Hampton boys dropping by, too, aren't I?"

"I hope so." She reached across the table and squeezed his hand. Warmth radiated from her like sunbeams, warming him all the way through.

A slender young man with a mustache stepped up to their table, and Connor recognized him as the waiter who had served at Lorna's dinner party.

"André!" Sarah exclaimed with cheery welcome.

"Sarah, I thought that was you," André replied with a French cadence in his voice. "You look—" he lifted his shoulders in a uniquely Continental shrug "—*magnifique.*"

She blushed and murmured thanks.

"I want to thank you for your advice about my bird," André continued. "I did what you said, and—*voilà*—she has stopped attacking my roommate and spitting on my nose."

"Spitting on your nose?" Connor repeated.

In a discreetly lowered voice, Sarah explained, "It actually involves more than spitting. It's part of a mating ritual. You see, the bird formed an emotional bond with—"

Connor held up a hand. "More than I wanted to know."

She laughed and turned to André. "I'm glad the suggestions worked. I'm sure Lulu will be happier, too."

André nodded, uttered a few more words and left them.

"Is Lulu his roommate, or his bird?" Connor asked.

"His cat."

They laughed, held hands and smiled into each other's eyes. Connor leaned across the table and kissed her.

When their kiss had ended, Sarah whispered with a self-conscious glance around, "People are watching us."

"They're not used to seeing me kiss anyone." He ignored the stares angled their way. "I'm usually a private kind of guy."

"Then why are you kissing me now?"

"I can't help it," he answered truthfully, then kissed her again. "Besides, I want to make my intentions known."

She raised her brows playfully. "And just what are your intentions, sir?"

To marry you. There was no doubt left in his heart. He wanted her with him always, as his wife, his partner, his lover. The mother of his children. Nothing else seemed quite as important as winning her.

Yet, he couldn't tell her. He hadn't missed the uneasiness in her eyes that morning when he'd said she belonged to him. He had to move slowly, cautiously, or risk scaring her away. "My intentions," he replied, "are to keep you safe and happy...and with me."

Tenderness warmed her gaze, and he knew he couldn't kiss her then, or he really would make a spectacle of them.

They finished their lunch and walked to the bank, where he signed papers that the clerk had waiting for him. As they left the bank, Connor handed her an ATM card. "Use as much money as you want. All of it in that account is yours."

She remained strangely silent as they walked to his office and around the building to the back door. She then lifted a tear-shiny gaze to him. "I'll pay you back every penny of this loan, with interest. And I'll be the best housekeeper you've ever had. I'll—"

"Sarah." He took hold of her slender shoulders and gently shook her. "I'm not in this for a payback of any kind. Not even your gratitude. God—" he murmured more to himself than her "—*especially* not your gratitude." He could so easily mistake it for love. Was that the emotion he saw in her gaze— gratitude?

Her eyes swam with unshed tears. "I just want

to show you how much I appreciate everything you're doing for me."

Feeling somewhat desperate at the thought that her tenderness and passion could spring from mere gratitude, he whispered fiercely, "Then promise me something, Sarah. Promise you won't leave without talking it over with me first."

"I wouldn't do that!"

"Swear it."

"I swear." Overwhelmed by the deep, chaotic emotion she felt for him, Sarah sealed the vow with a devout kiss. He pulled her closer, and they leaned against the brick building to prolong the contact for another few needful moments.

Before he let her go, he gruffly reminded her, "Don't take off that dress. I want to do it."

With a smile on her lips, love in her heart and a sweet, hot desire in her blood, she did as she was told.

By THE END of that week, Sarah believed she thoroughly knew Connor. They'd spent every moment they could together—making love, laughing, rescuing Tofu from the dreary local pound and quietly enjoying each other's company.

While the shaggy black-and-white dog scampered about the house and yard, Sarah and Connor shared home-cooked suppers and cozy evenings by the fire, deep in conversation. He'd told her about his hectic college days, his two restless years in Boston and his relief at moving back to Sugar Falls.

It was with some surprise, then, that she discovered a hidden side to him. She'd unpacked the boxes stacked in the guest bedrooms, putting away towels, blankets, clothing and kitchen utensils. Behind the boxes, she'd found chairs, a desk and end tables, which she'd set up in various rooms of the house.

She then started on the crates in the upstairs "bonus" room, which he hadn't mentioned. She wouldn't have known it was there if she hadn't mistaken its door for a closet.

The unpacking of those crates turned into a dig for treasure as she uncovered the most exquisite hand carvings, pottery, paintings and tapestries. Many of the pieces were signed by "Deidre Wade" and "Sutton Wade." She guessed that they'd been his parents.

She then discovered a guitar, a tambourine, a harmonica, a flute and a stereo system. More surprising still, she came across audiotapes with handwritten labels. Most of the songs were written and performed by Sutton Wade.

One tape featured songs by Connor Wade.

She set up the stereo system in Connor's living room, then played the tapes. His voice, music and lyrics touched her deeply. He'd been a teenager at the time, she guessed. The music combined the driving beat and soulful guitar of modern rock with the haunting lyrics of a folk ballad. He'd captured in the songs a young man's passionate need for self-discovery.

In a couple of songs, he was accompanied by a deeper, gruffer voice. From the other tapes, she recognized the voice as Sutton Wade's. His father's.

Sarah found herself crying for no good reason.

She spent that entire Thursday afternoon listening to the music and decorating the house with Connor's parents' art. She became so involved in her odyssey through his secret past that she lost track of the time. She hadn't even started cooking supper when Tofu's bark alerted her that Connor was home.

She met him at the front door.

The first thing he noticed was her face. "You've been crying." He gathered her to him in concern. "What's wrong?"

"Nothing." She smiled and kissed him. "I was just so...moved."

"'Moved'?"

It was then that he noticed the tapestry she'd draped across the wall of his living room...the pottery she'd placed on his mantel...the paintings and carvings that now graced every possible space.

She waited in breathless expectation for his reaction. The art had added so much warmth and personality to the house that she almost expected to see his eyes fill with tears as hers had.

"Take it down."

She blinked. "Pardon me?"

His face had frozen into stiff lines. "I'm selling all this to a dealer in Denver."

"Selling it! But wasn't it your parents' art?"

A troublesome emotion flickered through his eyes, then was quickly gone. "Go to any store in town, charge anything to my account, decorate the house to your heart's content. But put all this away." He headed for the back door without even changing from his work clothes. "I'm going riding. I'd like everything down by the time I come home."

She followed him through the kitchen, hurt and bewildered by his cold reaction. "What about the tapes? Your father's music, and...and yours. Do I have to pack those up, too?"

He swung back to her abruptly. "You found the tapes?"

She nodded, unsure how he'd react.

"Give them to me."

She knew, without a doubt, that he'd destroy them. She shook her head. "No."

"No?" he repeated, incredulous.

"That's right." She raised her chin. "No."

"Sarah, I want the tapes."

"So do I. I want the art, too. I'll buy it all from you. It might take me a while to pay for it, but I—"

"Damn it, Sarah, you can't have any of it," he thundered. "It has nothing to do with you."

"But it has a lot to do with you," she shouted right back at him, "or you wouldn't be this upset!"

With an anger she'd never seen in him before, he strode from the house. Furious, she snatched every blessed piece of art down from the walls, shelves and mantel, carried it upstairs to the packing crates and then locked herself in the guest bedroom.

She lay on the bed and cuddled Tofu to her for comfort. It seemed an eternity before she heard a knock at her door.

"Sarah," Connor called out, "I'm sorry."

She didn't answer. He'd hurt her, and she wanted him to know it. *This has nothing to do with you*," he'd said. He couldn't have told her more clearly that she wasn't welcome in the private areas of his heart.

"I was wrong," he admitted hoarsely. "I shouldn't have yelled, or walked out."

She sat up on the bed and let the dog scamper from her embrace. Neither of the things Connor had mentioned bothered her as much as his refusal to share his feelings.

"Open the door, Sarah. Please." He sounded utterly weary. "None of the art or the tapes mean anything to me...but you do." In an almost inaudible whisper, he added, "You mean everything."

Her heart beat in her throat as she slowly rose from the bed and opened the door.

His eyes blazed with dark, tumultuous emotion.

"I don't need your ATM card," she said, "or free use of your stables, or the keys to your car. But damn it, Connor, I do need to understand *you*."

He pulled her into his arms and buried his face in her hair, holding her so tightly she could feel his inner turmoil.

She'd caused him pain, she realized. In her zeal to make him happy, she'd caused him pain. "Connor," she whispered, shaken by her own heedlessness, "I'm so sorry."

He took her face between his hands and kissed her as if he were drowning and she was his only salvation. She answered with a passion that awed her. He drew her down onto the cushions in front of the fireplace. Delving into long, emotion-charged kisses, they undressed each other.

He then pinned her beneath his naked, muscle-hard body, pressed her hands above her head and gazed deeply into her eyes as he made slow, hard love to her.

Her climax came from someplace deeper than it

ever had before, and left her hot, quaking and inexplicably needy.

She wanted to own him, heart and soul. When they were both able to stand, she led him from the living room to his bed, where she loved him in bold, new ways. She kissed him everywhere with long, languorous tastes, then concentrated her attention on his swollen tip, savoring for the first time the salty, male flavor of him.

"Sarah," he groaned, breaking into a sweat and grabbing for her shoulders, "you don't have to—"

"Shh." A feather-light flick of her tongue brought his hips off the bed. She whispered, "Just say 'ahhh....'"

He did, uncontrollably. When she'd goaded him into desperation, she straddled him, impaling herself with slow, sensuous undulations. Urgently he gripped her hips and thrust upward until every muscle in his glistening body strained and he cried out in a shuddering climax.

She knew she never had loved anyone else as she loved him. She needed no memories to be certain.

Later, as they lay sated, dreamy and exhausted in each other's arms, she asked him about his parents. She wanted to understand the pain she'd caused him earlier.

He began hesitantly, but soon lost himself in the telling.

"They met in San Francisco during the late sixties. Haight-Ashbury," he specified. "A place of epic significance." The lightly mocking inflection in his tone bewildered her. "They moved to a site just north of here with friends and started a colony for artists and musicians.

"They'd lived the 'natural way,' according to my father's definition—as vegetarians, pacifists and holistic healers. They spurned conventional medicine in favor of herbs, aromatherapy and—" he twisted his mouth at this "—flute music. Oh, and marijuana."

"Still, you became a traditional doctor," she noted with interest.

He squared his jaw, but didn't comment.

Sarah urged him on with questions, listening in fascination as he described his upbringing. For years, they'd lived without electricity until they'd learned about solar power. "My father approved of that. He considered it more 'natural.' And, it allowed him to play electric guitar and record his songs. Music," he explained, "was sacred."

"I could see that," she whispered. "I listened to yours."

Again, he didn't comment, but smoothly changed the subject. "My mother taught me and the other kids academic subjects. We rarely went into town—any of us—except to sell artwork."

"Then how did you attend high school in Sugar Falls?"

"By that time, I was old enough to rebel. I had to experience more of the world than just—" He broke off into tight-lipped silence. He obviously wasn't ready to share his feelings about his home.

"Did you know people in the town?"

"Not many. They'd all heard rumors about the 'hippies in the mountains.' Drug use, paganistic rituals, orgies."

"Were the rumors true?"

He slanted her an uneasy glance. "Not all of them."

She realized then how mortified he'd been by the townspeople's view of him. He'd been a boy in a town full of strangers, made to feel ashamed of his family and his past.

"Once I came to understand how most of society lived," he continued, "there was no going back. I felt like I'd been liberated."

Funny, she thought, how one man's freedom could be another man's prison. "It must have been hard for you during high school," she mused, "socially and academically."

He didn't reply.

"Did you travel down from your home every day?"

"No. I rented a room from Gladys."

"Gladys, your nurse?" she asked in surprise.

He nodded. "She's the one who first got me interested in the medical profession and guided me through the rough spots."

Sarah thought back to Gladys's vehement defense of him during her first visit to his office, when she'd insisted he was one of the finest doctors to be found. Though she didn't know the petite, gray-haired lady at all, she already loved her.

"How did your parents feel about your venturing out into the world?"

The stiffness returned to his face; the shutters drew over his eyes. "Betrayed."

Gently, almost fearfully, she asked, "Did you ever go back?"

"Not while my parents were alive."

Her heart bled for him.

After a long pause, he said, "My father died from appendicitis during my first year in med school. I wrote to my mother and tried to get her to move into town. She secretly wanted to, for as long as I could remember. But she wouldn't. Said she felt closer to my father in their home." He shook his head grimly. "A few months later, she died of exposure in a snowstorm." He met her gaze, and Sarah saw the pain for what it was. Grief. "They were crazy as hell. Both of them."

"I wish I could have known them," she whispered.

Disapproval twisted his mouth, and he looked as if he might chastise her. She raised her brows, daring him to.

He settled his head back against the pillow and grudgingly let out a laugh. "Something tells me they would have loved you."

Oddly enough, she believed he meant it as a compliment.

Tofu barked sharply from the other room, and the doorbell rang. Connor and Sarah glanced at each other in surprise, then at the clock. It was only nine, but felt much later.

"Who the hell—?" muttered Connor. Quickly he donned his jeans while Sarah shrugged into his large terry-cloth robe. She lingered in the hallway and curiously watched as Connor headed for the door with Tofu prancing at his heels.

"Annie!" Connor greeted in surprise.

"Annie?" cried Sarah, hurrying forward as her friend, mentor and rescuing angel stepped into the living room.

The petite redhead caught her in a tight hug.

"Sarah, honey, how are you?" She searched her face with motherly concern. "I was so worried about you. I called you at Lorna's house yesterday, and was told that you no longer worked there. Ted and I came home right away. I was so afraid you'd be holed up in some hotel somewhere, if you even had the money for that." She glanced from a shirtless Connor to a robe-clad Sarah, and her freckled face reddened. "Seems you found a place, though."

Sarah ignored the warmth rising in her own cheeks. "I told you not to worry about me. I'm fine. Connor has been—" the warmth in her face deepened as she glanced at him "—wonderful."

"Uh, yeah," Annie replied. "I've heard that."

Connor's hazel eyes twinkled in amused response.

"So, Sarah," asked Annie, her voice sounding a little strained, "has there been anything...new?"

From the concerned undertone in Annie's voice, Sarah realized she meant memory-wise. "It's okay to talk in front of Connor," she said. "He knows everything. And yes, a few memories have come back, but nothing to tell me who I am."

"At least the memories have begun to return."

"Have a seat, Annie," Connor invited, gesturing toward the chairs Sarah had arranged in his living room. "I'll make coffee."

"No, I'm not going to stay. I just wanted to tell Sarah something that might be important." The anxious look that had come over her face drew Sarah's concerned attention.

With a slight pull of foreboding, she asked, "What is it?"

"A stranger called my house, looking for you."

"For me?"

"He said he tracked my name and number down through the hospital billing system. He knew that I paid the bills for a patient named Sarah who had suffered amnesia after an accident."

Sarah's heart began to pound. Connor slid his arm around her, his expression entirely sober now.

"It seems that a woman he's looking for had disappeared the same day that you were admitted to the hospital. A woman named Sarah." Annie bit her lip nervously, her cheeks flushed, her eyes anxious. "He described you perfectly. I was afraid to tell him anything about you, though, because you swore me to secrecy. I knew you were afraid that someone was after you...so I told him I didn't know what had happened to you after you were discharged."

Sarah swayed on her feet, feeling suddenly disoriented. Connor tightened his arm and lodged her firmly against him. "Did you get his name," she asked, "and phone number?"

"I couldn't ask for his number after I said I didn't know anything about you!" exclaimed Annie. "But I did get the number he was calling from. I have a caller-identification box on my phone, you know."

"Who was he, Annie?" Sarah clutched Connor's hand. "What was his name?"

"Jack," she replied. "Jack Forrester."

Jack. The name she'd said in her sleep.

"Did he say the name of the woman he's looking for?" Sarah inquired in a shaky whisper.

"He said she could be going under the name Sarah Myers," Annie replied, "or, Sarah Myers Tierney."

9

"DO EITHER OF THOSE NAMES feel familiar, Sarah?" asked Annie.

Sarah squeezed her hands together. "I've always felt that my first name was Sarah," she whispered faintly, "and the name Myers has a...familiar feel to it. But—" She shook her head.

Sarah Myers. She supposed it was possible.

Sarah Myers Tierney. The very sound made her feel sick. So did the name Jack Forrester. She didn't remember the man at all, but the name sent shivers of unease down her spine. Why would he have given two possible names for her?

"Let me see the number he called from." Connor took the paper that Annie handed to him.

"Don't call that number," Sarah cried. "If he was the one who chased me before the accident, he might trace our call." The fear she'd felt during her nightmares seeped back into her bones, as if her phantom pursuer had reached out and touched her. "He'd know where to find us."

"Us." She'd brought her problems into the lives of both Annie and Connor. Was she endangering them?

"Sarah, sweetheart, calm down." Connor slid his arm around her and pulled her comfortingly close. "I'm not going to call the number. I'm going to give it to the detective I hired yesterday, along with the names Jack Forrester and Sarah Myers Tierney. He can check them both out for us. That can't hurt, can it?"

She released a rush of breath. "I suppose not."

He hugged her to him as he dialed the phone.

Unable to withstand the anxiety building in her, Sarah broke away and paced across the living room.

"I guess I'll leave you two to handle this," said Annie, her face creased with worry. "Let me know whatever the detective finds out, or if you remember anything more."

Sarah thanked her for bringing the news and for withholding all information from the stranger. She then stood at the front door and watched as Annie hurried to her car.

Staring into the cool springtime darkness long after Annie's headlights had vanished, Sarah faced the obvious possibility that everyone had thoughtfully refrained from mentioning—that "Myers" could be her maiden name. Which would make "Tierney" her married name.

No. There had to be another explanation.

She closed the door and wrapped her arms around herself, feeling suddenly cold.

Connor finished his discussion with the detective and turned to Sarah. "He's going to dial the number to see who answers. He'll be calling me back any minute. Tomorrow he'll check out the names. At least we have something to go on now."

She uttered a vague response, trying to sound optimistic.

The phone rang, and Connor answered. After a

few brief words, he hung up, looking disappointed. "The number turned out to be a pay phone at the hospital in Denver."

"A pay phone! So we have nothing."

"It was a long-distance call. He may have charged it to a card or another phone. We also have the name Jack Forrester—if it's his real name. And, most important of all, we have the name Sarah Myers Tierney."

Sarah found little comfort in any of it.

Connor pulled her into his arms, cradled her against his chest and stroked her hair. "For now, let's try to relax, okay? We'll get through this, Sarah. You'll see."

She nodded and forced a smile. He kissed her.

Though she allowed him to usher her back to bed, she didn't sleep. The names resounded in a wearisome litany through her head. Jack Forrester. Sarah Myers Tierney. Sarah Myers.

Fatigue pressed down on her. As she began to nod off to sleep, a memory jogged her back into wakefulness. *Aunt Martha Myers.* Her aunt! She clearly saw the image of her face, her neat white hair, her favorite gray cardigan, her gentle smile.

Sarah sat up in the bed. How could she have forgotten Aunt Martha? She'd been the only mother she'd known since...

Memories surfaced in scattered bits. She vaguely remembered her parents and their death in an auto accident when she was a child. She'd lived with Aunt Martha until she moved into her own apartment. In Tallahassee! She'd lived in Tallahassee, Florida.

Leaning back against the pillows, she sifted

through the tenuous strands of memories that filtered through the fog in her brain. She recalled random events and people from her childhood, high school and college days. Other details escaped her, though. Too many details. She remembered nothing about her adult life, Jack Forrester or the name "Tierney." Had it been her name?

With a glance at Connor, who had fallen into a deep sleep, she gently disengaged herself from his embrace, climbed out of bed and crept into the living room. It was shortly before midnight. Too late to call the East Coast.

But she had to.

She dialed directory assistance for Tallahassee. "Martha Myers, please, on Lakeshore Drive." She scrawled the number on a paper Connor had left near the phone.

Her heart sped up. She could know everything with one call. Surely Aunt Martha would know all the important things. Swallowing her inexplicable trepidation, she dialed.

After many rings, a sleepy, warbly feminine voice answered.

Warm tears filled Sarah's eyes. "Aunt Martha, it's Sarah."

"Sarah? Oh, sweet heavens, Sarah! Where are you?"

"Colorado."

"I've been worried silly. Why haven't you called me? It's been so long. And every time I call you, I reach an answering machine. I've left so many messages."

"I'm sorry, Aunt Martha. I was in an accident."

"An accident? Oh, no. Sarah, honey..."

"I'm all right now," she hurriedly assured her, "except that I...I can't remember some things."

"'Can't remember'? Oh, my! That sounds serious. Why in heaven's name didn't Grant call me?"

"Grant?" she replied faintly. "Who's Grant?"

A short silence followed the question.

"You mean, you don't know?" her aunt asked incredulously. "Oh, my, my. You're not home, then? You're not with him?"

Sarah gripped the phone tightly. *Home. With him.* She didn't like the sound of that. "Tell me who he is. Please."

"He's your husband, dear."

Dread rose up to choke her. *Your husband.*

She suddenly pictured a face to go with the name—a classically handsome face with wide-set blue eyes and a dimpled smile. Dark, wavy hair. An infectious laugh. Elegance, old-world charm... fairy-tale romance...

Her aunt droned on about how lavishly Grant had courted her; how he worshiped the ground she walked on; how his corporate business had forced them to move to Colorado. Sarah heard only a word here and there. She was too overwhelmed.

Grant Tierney. He'd been the one pushing the wedding band onto her left hand. She remembered little else about him.

Closing her eyes, she forced words through a painfully tight throat. "Were you at my wedding, Aunt Martha?"

"Heavens, no. My doctor won't let me travel that far."

"Did I talk to you after the wedding?"

"Not even once! I waited and waited. I figured

you were on your honeymoon, but two months is an awfully long time, even for a man with as much money as Grant."

"I need his phone number. Grant's phone number...and address."

"My goodness, Sarah, you really don't remember them?" It took a while for Aunt Martha to understand how that could be, then another few minutes to find the information.

As she read it aloud, Sarah copied it down.

"One more question, Aunt Martha. Do you know a man named Jack Forrester?"

"Jack Forrester. Hmm. I don't believe so." After a pensive moment, she asked anxiously, "You'll be okay, won't you, dear? I think you should get on the next plane and come home to me until you're well again. Honey and Spice miss you, you know. You remember them, don't you? You were supposed to send for them, once you were settled."

"Thank you for keeping them, Aunt Martha," she murmured. "I'll call you again tomorrow."

She hung up the phone in a daze.

"Sarah?" Connor's deep, sleep-husky voice reverberated from the hallway. "Were you on the phone?"

Not trusting her voice, she nodded.

"Who were you talking to?"

"My aunt," she whispered.

"Your aunt?" With a sleepy squint, he trudged into the living room and sank down into the chair beside hers. "You remembered her?"

Again, she nodded.

He opened his eyes wider, wholly alert now. "What did she tell you?"

Though she tried to answer, the words stuck in her throat.

"Sarah." He frowned and leaned forward. "Tell me what she said."

"I'm married."

He stared at her in thunderstruck silence.

"To a man named Grant Tierney." Her voice shook, and she waited for a moment to steady it. It emerged in a raspy whisper. "I remember him. I remember...marrying him."

Silence throbbed between them.

He shut his eyes. His chest slowly expanded as he inhaled deeply. He sat very still in his chair.

She tried not to think. At all. Not now. Maybe not ever.

"It's late," he finally uttered in a tight, unrecognizable voice. "We...aren't thinking clearly." He opened his eyes. They looked bleak and dazed. "We'll talk about this tomorrow."

Rising from the chair, he held his hand out to her. She took it. Together they moved toward his bedroom.

His bedroom. A flood of realization washed through her. She dropped his hand and halted in the hallway.

He swung an uncomprehending glance at her. Like a match struck into flame, understanding flared in his eyes.

She couldn't sleep with him. Of course she couldn't sleep with him. *She was married to another man.*

"I don't believe," he whispered, "that you could have made love to me the way you did—" his throat contracted in a hard swallow; a muscle moved in his jaw "—if you loved another man. Even if you didn't remember him." His stare was hot enough to brand her.

She didn't reply. But in her heart, she had to agree.

He turned and strode to his bedroom. Alone.

BEFORE THE SUN ROSE, Sarah hooked Tofu to a leash, walked him into town with her and called Grant Tierney from a pay phone. She couldn't quite think of Grant as her husband.

She'd never made love to anyone but Connor. Her body, heart and soul had burned for him alone. She loved him—intensely, as she'd love no other.

But she'd married someone else.

She didn't want to believe it; didn't want to face up to it. She had to, though. She had to return to the man she'd married and do her best to remember their relationship. Only when she understood herself and the life she'd once led could she move forward in any direction at all.

She'd lain awake most of the night fighting her own demons. Pain and dread had stormed through her, along with the nameless fear. An inner voice issued vague warnings—or maybe memories—of danger.

Why? Could the fear simply be a symptom of the head trauma? Maybe so. But in case it wasn't, she couldn't risk drawing anyone else into the danger. She had to protect both Annie and Connor from becoming too involved in her problems. She had to face her past without them.

She wouldn't make the call to Grant Tierney

from Connor's house. She didn't want his number caught on a caller-identification box, or traced from an outside location.

Don't you trust the man you married? she asked herself.

How could she? She had no idea who it was she actually feared, or whom she'd run from. And she remembered so little about Grant Tierney.

How, she wondered, did Jack Forrester fit into the picture? Was he some deranged stalker who had stolen her away after the ceremony? It could account for her virginal state. Had she then escaped and run from him?

A recorded greeting answered, and she recognized Grant Tierney's voice. Snatches of memories played through her mind—dancing with Grant, sitting next to him on a private jet, dining in an expensive foreign restaurant. On the French Riviera, she believed it had been. She'd been having fun...and she'd been so flattered that a man like Grant would fall in love with her.

She remembered kissing him. A pleasant experience, if memory served correctly, but nothing remotely similar to the blood-stirring passion she'd felt with Connor.

She shut her eyes and gripped the phone. She couldn't think about Connor now. The wound was too raw; the pain too great.

She'd have to leave him. Today.

"Grant," she said into the receiver after the recorded beep had sounded, "this is Sarah. I...I'm coming...home." How odd it seemed, calling any place "home" other than Connor's house. She swallowed a sudden swelling in her throat. "I should be there by late this afternoon."

She hung up the phone and leaned against the brick front of the convenience store, nearly overcome by the pain of leaving. She couldn't afford to feel too deeply. She had to be guided by reason, not emotion. She had to discover her "real life."

At least the memories of Grant reassured her. She remembered him as a gentle, charming man who often made her laugh. Surely he could not have caused the fear.

Even as she thought of it, the fear zigzagged through her like lightning. She pressed her fist to her heart and concentrated on regaining her composure before she made her next call.

Drawing in a deep breath, she called Annie and asked for a ride into Denver. She intended to have Annie drive her just so far, and then she'd send her back to Sugar Falls. She'd take a cab the rest of the way to Grant's house.

She wouldn't let Annie anywhere near Grant's house until she remembered and understood entirely what had taken place after her wedding ceremony...and why her fear had grown by leaps and bounds since she'd heard the names Jack Forrester and Grant Tierney.

She could very well be walking back into some kind of dreadful problem. That was exactly why she wouldn't ask Connor to drive her to Denver. Connor wouldn't allow her to take a cab the rest of the way. At the very least, he'd follow her.

Panic touched her at the very thought. *He'd be hurt. Gravely hurt. Any man who helped her would be terribly, terribly hurt....*

Why, she wondered wildly, did she believe such a thing? As much as she'd tried to analyze that fear and reason it away, the certainty of it had only grown stronger until it squeezed her heart like a vise.

She would not allow Connor to become involved. She had to handle the situation—whatever it was—in her own way, without him. She'd have to make a clean break from him for his own protection.

She could leave while he was at work, she supposed, except she'd promised to tell him before she left. He'd been too good to her; too kind and caring. He'd asked her for only that promise in return. She couldn't possibly break it.

She'd have to tell him she was leaving. She'd have to make him believe that she'd be fine, that she wasn't frightened, that a loving husband awaited her.

Perhaps he did.

Determined to resist the tears that clogged her throat, she called Annie, who promised to do anything she could to help her. Sarah then returned home—or to Connor's house, she painfully corrected herself.

She found him pacing across the kitchen, the phone pressed to his ear, his handsome face set in grim, anxious lines. Her heart turned over at the sight of him. He was dressed in a dark shirt, jeans and soft leather boots; he looked strong, virile and eminently protective. She wanted to kiss him and hold him forever.

She loved him so damn much!

That was why she had to leave this house without him.

He set down the phone as she walked into the kitchen. "Where the hell were you?" Relief flashed in his troubled gaze. "God, Sarah, when I found you gone, I didn't know what to think. I was about to call the sheriff and go out looking myself."

"I took Tofu for a walk." She stopped a safe distance away from him and grasped the edge of the kitchen counter for support. *Be strong,* she told herself. *Be convincing.* "I'm leaving today."

He stared at her in grim silence.

"I, uh, already have my suitcase packed."

His mouth tightened. He crossed his muscular arms, lodged a shoulder against the refrigerator and steadily regarded her. "I saw that."

"I've asked Annie to drive me into Denver. To my, uh—" her voice wavered slightly "—my house there."

"You remembered where you lived?"

"Yes."

"You're not afraid to return there?"

"No. I'm sure now that the fear was groundless."

Connor forced himself to remain where he was. He couldn't touch her now. Couldn't pull her into his arms as he so often had. "I'd like to drive you, Sarah. I want to be sure you get there safely, and that everything's okay once you do."

"No. My…husband…will be waiting there for me."

The pain that had been gripping his heart since last night now tightened to an almost unbearable pressure. "You remember him clearly, then? You remember your relationship?"

"I do." She glanced away from him, her face growing paler than it had been. "And it would be awkward if you brought me home. I'm not quite ready to tell him about...about us."

"*About us.*" She'd made it sound like a tawdry affair. Was that how she saw the time they'd spent together and the love they'd made?

He'd been her first. Her only.

Unable to stop himself, he ventured closer until he stood near enough to touch her. To kiss her. God, he needed to. He needed to remind her of the emotion that powered every one of their kisses. "Do you love him?"

"Yes."

A deep, black chasm opened in his heart. The sharp, stunning pain of it cost him a few moments' breath. What had he been hoping for? That she'd leave her husband, the man she'd never slept with, the man who hadn't issued any bulletins for her or contacted any authorities? *Yes.*

"There are things," he whispered raggedly, "that I don't understand. Questions that I—"

"Connor," she reprimanded, silencing him with the sharpness of her tone. "Please believe that I know the answers to all those questions, and I'm satisfied with them. I simply don't feel it would be right to—" her breath briefly caught "—to share them with you."

The pain in him intensified.

Regret flickered among the emotions churning in her eyes. He swore he saw love there, too. Was he deluding himself? "I owe you a lot for your help," she said, "and your...your kindness." Her chin quivered, but she went on, "I'll always be grateful."

"*Grateful.*"

"But I need to put my life back together," she whispered.

Her life. She'd found her life, and it didn't include him. He couldn't fault her for that. She was the one acting honorably now; not him. He had to get it through his head that she was married. Another man's wife.

A fine sheen welled up in her beautiful gray eyes, the ones he'd gazed so deeply into while he'd made love to her. "I want to make my marriage work," she said.

He felt the darkness reaching for him—from the cold, hollow depths of the chasm that had once been his heart. "Okay," he heard himself say. "Let me know if you need anything. I'll be at my office." He turned to leave while he still could.

"Connor," she cried, stopping him at the living-room door.

He braced himself and turned back to her.

"I'm sorry." A tear slipped from the corner of her eye and trickled past her mouth. "I never meant to hurt you."

In that gut-wrenching moment, while emotion held them both in its cruel grip, he was strongly tempted to kiss her, tell her how much he loved her, tell her that he'd die inside without her. He wanted her more than he'd ever wanted anything in his life, and he'd always gone after what he wanted.

But she loved someone else. She wanted her

marriage to work. He couldn't willingly destroy it. Even if, by some miracle, she agreed to stay with him, he didn't want her to sacrifice the love she'd vowed to keep sacred. He loved her too much to do that to her.

And he could never settle for her fondness, her gratitude, or her physical passion. He wanted her love...which belonged to someone else.

"You didn't hurt me, Sarah," he softly assured her. "I'll miss you, of course, but..." He ran out of voice, so he lifted a shoulder in a negligent shrug until he found a whisper to replace it with. "We both knew you'd be leaving when you found your...your life." He believed he even managed a small smile. "I've got my life to keep me busy, too."

She bit her bottom lip until it turned white.

He dragged his gaze away from her mouth—the mouth another man would be kissing.

He had to leave before he exploded.

DRESSED IN AN ECRU LINEN vest and a flowing floral-print skirt, Sarah loaded her suitcase into Annie's trunk and left Connor's house shortly before noon.

The pain of leaving him was excruciating. She sat in silence for most of the two-hour drive to Denver, her throat muscles stiff and aching from holding back tears.

It had taken every ounce of her strength to utter the lies she'd told him. She didn't love the man she remembered as her husband. She would never love anyone but Connor.

He apparently didn't love her in the same way.

"You didn't hurt me, Sarah," he'd said. *"I'll miss you, of course, but…"* For her, there were no buts. She would miss him from the bottom of her soul. Nothing or no one would fill the void.

What had she expected from him? Men like Connor didn't take strange women into their homes with the intention of keeping them forever. She'd done exactly what Mimsey had insinuated; she'd taken his kindness for more than it had been. Oh, they'd shared some good times, and heart-to-heart talks, and long, wonderful hours of lovemaking. But he'd never meant for her to take their relationship as anything more than temporary. He'd said it himself. "We both knew you'd be leaving when you found your life. I've got my life to keep me busy, too."

She felt as if her heart had been ripped out of her.

"Sarah, are you sure you're ready to go back to your husband?" Annie asked, slanting her a worried glance from the driver's seat.

"Oh, definitely," Sarah replied, striving to hit an upbeat note. "It's high time I got my life back in order." She forced a smile. "It's such a relief to know who I am and where I…I belong." Her throat, unfortunately, had chosen to close up on the last word, choking her into silence.

Annie bit her lip and furrowed her brow as she drove.

They reached Denver around two-thirty. Neither of them was in a particular hurry to say goodbye. They stopped for a late lunch at a downtown café, discussing many of the memories that had returned to Sarah.

She mentioned Grant Tierney, of course, and related the details she remembered. She did not mention the gaping holes that remained in her memory regarding her relationship with Grant, or the inexplicable fear that continued to haunt her.

"I'm so relieved, Sarah, that you know who you are and that you remember your husband." Annie's gaze probed her face. "I must admit, though, that I was surprised this morning when you told me you were ready to go back to him. It just seems so abrupt. When I saw you with Connor last night, I felt so sure that the two of you..." She blushed and looked away.

Pain throbbed in Sarah's chest. "I have to do what's right," she whispered.

Annie nodded and changed the subject. Sarah was glad. She couldn't talk about Connor right now.

She had to concentrate instead on the present and the future. Both were inescapably tied to the man she barely remembered. Grant Tierney.

If she'd loved him enough to marry him, why did she dread seeing him again or venturing near his house? The fear could be a symptom of the head trauma, she reminded herself. Was it?

"Are you sure I can't drive you to your house?"

"Thanks, but no. My husband is meeting me at the airport," she lied. "I guess he'll be flying in from a business trip."

"Okay." Reluctantly, she glanced at her watch. "It's already four-thirty. Guess I'd better drive you to the airport, and head back to Sugar Falls."

The drive was too short for Sarah's liking. They arrived at the airport in no time at all.

"I'll miss you, kiddo," Annie croaked, her blue

eyes clouding with tears. "You'll call me, won't you? We'll visit and keep in touch?"

"Always." They hugged, cried, laughed at each other and whispered their goodbyes.

Sarah watched as Annie drove away. How she hated to see her go! She wished so much that Annie could be the one to drive her to Grant Tierney's house. She desperately needed her emotional support to see her through this upcoming ordeal.

But the fear that pounded through her at the thought of returning to Grant wouldn't allow her to involve Annie. She had to face this reunion alone.

Gathering her courage, she picked up her suitcase, resolutely walked to a pay phone and called a cab.

SHE'D GONE. SHE REALLY had gone.

He'd had no doubt that she would leave, yet a stubborn hope had stayed with Connor throughout the morning that she might still be there when he got home. He closed the clinic at noon, needing to see her. That hope was laid to rest when he returned home to find only a yapping little Shih Tzu waiting for him and a note taped to the refrigerator.

The note reiterated how grateful Sarah would always be and how much she'd enjoyed her stay. She expressed hope that he'd want to keep Tofu. She would have felt guilty taking the dog away from where Timmy and Jeffrey could visit him, and she believed that Connor himself had grown fond of the pup.

She promised to repay the money she'd borrowed. She wished him a very happy life.

Connor changed into his jeans, saddled up Viking and rode hard, fast and long. He couldn't, of course, outride the pain. The pain sliced deep into his heart, and he marveled that he could still breathe or move or think.

Not that he wanted to think. Thinking only increased the pain, because every thought was somehow linked to Sarah. Her scent, her feel, her essence, hovered around him in the very air, yet remained infinitely beyond his reach.

He rode mindlessly, urging the stallion farther up the mountain until the slopes grew rocky, the trees stunted, the air colder and thinner. He brought the horse to a halt, tied him to a bare, dwarfed tree, then walked off into a wasteland of jagged crevices, rust-colored boulders and bottomless canyons.

The pain had built to an unbearable pressure in his chest. He'd never have her again, never hold her, never laugh with her or gaze into her eyes. He'd found the woman he loved, and she belonged to someone else.

He stopped at a canyon's edge and let out a deep, hoarse, primal yell. The pain, the anger, the hopelessness, echoed back to him a dozen times. He yelled again, and again, then sank down onto a boulder, shut his eyes and allowed the pain to wash through him in scalding currents.

He would have given anything to win her love. He would have walked away from the life he'd worked for, from everything he'd become, if that was what it would have taken to make her happy.

He'd fallen too deeply in love. She'd become an addiction. A potentially lethal addiction. He'd needed her as badly as alcoholics need a drink; as smokers need a smoke; as junkies need a fix. As badly, he realized, as his parents had needed their godforsaken mountains.

Badly enough to die for.

He swallowed spasmodically and forced himself to breathe. He'd never thought he'd fall into such a trap. He'd lived his life with the utmost caution, making choices based on logic. He'd charted a course for himself when he'd been just a boy and hadn't strayed from it…until he'd fallen in love with another man's wife.

He'd never felt as lost or alone as he did right now.

He glanced around, knowing he needed to put his emotions into perspective. With dull surprise, he recognized where he was. He hadn't been to this particular ledge for at least seventeen years.

He had come here often with his father. Many an hour they'd spent, just the two of them, gazing over these jagged cliffs, talking and thinking and sometimes playing guitar.

A different pain sliced through his heart—this one older and sheathed in anger. He couldn't think of his father or his mother without that stabbing anger. They'd denied him the freedom they professed to love. They'd scorned his vocation—medical science itself—choosing to believe in herbs, chants and the curative powers of flute music. They'd refused to see reason, to move into town, to join the world.

He'd needed the world. He'd needed its good

opinion of him. He hadn't understood how they could not.

As he glared out into the cool mist, he realized with a sense of shock that he understood now. Suddenly, clearly, he understood.

They'd had each other. They'd had their dreams. They'd lived the life they'd chosen and had died on their own terms. Why hadn't he seen the nobility in that?

Had they ever come to understand *him?* He'd spent so much of his young adulthood breaking his ties to them; disassociating himself from their lifestyle. Even when he'd returned from Boston, he'd kept their art and music locked away, determined to keep even the memories of them at bay.

Sarah hadn't understood. She'd adorned his home with the free-spirited beauty that had been his parents. The shock had been more than he could hide. He'd felt as if he'd stepped back in time; as if he could call out their names and they'd look up from their artwork and gesture for him to join them.

The aching loss he'd felt had angered him. He'd thought he'd left that pain far, far behind. He'd thought he'd left *them* far, far behind.

He knew now that he hadn't. They were a part of him. At one time, that fact would have mortified him. It no longer did. What had once seemed like flaws in his parents, he now saw as strengths.

Sarah had seen that before he had.

But he couldn't think of Sarah. Much easier to focus on the old pain, the one he'd lived with for so long. He'd learned to deal with the anger, the shame, the betrayal he'd felt over his parents by simply putting them out of his life. He would live with the grief of missing them and the shame of abandoning them until the day he died.

But he wasn't sure he could live with the pain he felt over losing Sarah. Exist, yes. Live, no. He'd been hollowed out, like the crevices in these cold, rock mountains. Mountains that had been both his prison and his home. Mountains that he both hated and loved.

He'd been drawn back here—to the people of Sugar Falls, he'd thought. Yet he'd been ready to battle them all for Sarah's sake. He would gladly live without their good opinion, he realized, if he could have her by his side.

Even if he couldn't.

He peered out over the ledge, down into the gray-misted depths of the canyon. He visualized his parents' faces, heard the music they'd made, marveled at the colors they'd wielded like bright, powerful magic. That magic had once comprised his whole world.

He would need the part of his soul he'd left behind in these old mountains. He would need every blessed fragment of his soul to help him get through the rest of his life.

As he let the pain flow through him and cauterize old wounds, the wind rushed through the rocks in an eerie melody.

It sounded strangely like flute music.

10

CONNOR RETURNED FROM THE stables around three that afternoon to find a sleek, black Harley-Davidson parked in his front driveway. Curious as to who would be driving a Harley in Sugar Falls, he strode around the house, past the motorcycle, to the front porch.

A stranger stood knocking on his door. Dressed in black denim and leather, he looked like he might belong to some motorcycle gang. He stood about an inch taller than Connor with a solid build, muscular arms, shaggy blond hair and the beginnings of a beard glinting at his jaw. A fresh-looking scar disfigured one cheek, just below his eye.

What the hell did he want? Medical help of some kind, probably. Connor halted at the bottom of his porch steps and squinted up at the stranger through the midafternoon sun. "You looking for me?"

He turned and regarded Connor with surprisingly intelligent brown eyes. "You Doc Wade?"

Connor nodded and climbed the few steps to the porch.

"The name's Jack." The stranger extended a cordial hand. "Jack Forrester."

Every muscle in Connor's body tensed as he gripped the man's hand. Jack Forrester. Sarah's mysterious caller. The one she'd been afraid to call back. The one whose name she'd said in her sleep.

The stranger smiled, and despite his scar and scruffy clothing, Connor recognized him as a man women would go for. "I'm looking for a friend by the name of Sarah. A few folks in town told me you have a guest by that name. I'm wondering if she might be the one I'm looking for."

Connor inquired with deceptive softness, "And if she is, what do you want with her?"

"I have some private business to discuss with her."

"You went through a hell of a lot of trouble to find her, didn't you, Jack?"

"Some."

"Sure you just want to talk?"

The stranger's stance squared and his light brown gaze lit with challenge. "I'm not sure what business it is of yours, but yeah…I just want to talk."

Connor inched closer, eye-to-eye, ready to tear his head off at the first wrong move. "What makes you think the woman you're looking for is in Sugar Falls?"

"Annie Tompkins. She doesn't lie worth a damn. I figured she was hiding something, and came to see what it might be."

Connor caught the guy by his leather vest and shoved him up against the log wall of the cabin, his fists lodged at the base of his throat. "Somehow, Jack, I can't see Sarah having a friend like you, and I don't like the idea of you hunting her."

"Great," he muttered in a choked whisper. "Just great. I'd love to oblige you in a fight, pal, but I've already had a hole blown through me over this woman, and I'm not looking to have it busted open again."

"You were shot?" Connor tightened his hold. "By who?"

"Grant Tierney."

Foreboding trickled through Connor. Sarah's husband had actually shot the man? "Maybe he had good reason."

"If you believe that, you must not know him," Jack Forrester retorted. "He's one crazy bastard."

Something about the steadiness of the guy's gaze made Connor believe him. He released his grip. "Crazy, how?"

"Possessive. Obsessive. Just plain nuts. Of course, not too many people realize that. He puts on a good front." Jack Forrester straightened his stance, tugged at his leather vest and adjusted his shirt. A corner of a white bandage showed beneath his collarbone. He'd been shot pretty damn close to the heart....

"Are you saying Grant Tierney might hurt Sarah?"

Jack's eyes narrowed. "She didn't go back to him, did she?"

Connor gritted his teeth against the anxiety slamming through him. "Yes."

"Aw, hell!"

The two men stared at each other in grim silence.

"If you don't mind, Doc," Jack Forrester rumbled, "I could use something cold to drink. I'll answer any questions you have. And no, I'm not stalking her or making a play for her."

"Damn good thing." Shoving open the door of

his cabin, Connor led the way to the kitchen. He tossed Jack a bottle of cold spring water, impatient to get all the information he could. Jack sat on a stool at the breakfast bar and guzzled the water.

"Tell me everything," Connor urged, "and make it quick."

"I only met her a couple of times. Once in an airport when I ran into Grant, and another time at a picnic on the Point."

"The Point?"

"Moccasin Point, Florida. Grant and I grew up there."

Connor frowned. "You grew up with Grant Tierney?"

"He lived next door to me. His mother still does. Anyway, Grant's always been a little crazy when it comes to women. You see, he has this thing for, uh—" he tossed Connor an uncomfortable glance "—virgins."

Coldness shot through Connor. "What kind of 'thing'?"

"He's really into the idea of being 'the only one.' He insists on having a virgin bride. Of course, I don't know if Sarah's a virgin, but from the way Grant feels about the subject, I'd assume so."

Connor didn't have to assume. He knew. His hands balled into fists. "He actually talked to you about this?"

"He brought it up now and then, when we used to be friends. That was before I realized how crazy he is." A dark, tense look came over Jack's face. "Before he married my sister."

"Your sister!"

"He made her life a living hell. It took years of

therapy for her to get over it. After she left him, he married another woman, who also divorced him. Then he met Sarah."

Connor's hands tightened into fists. The thought of Sarah with a man like that made his gut hurt. "Why don't the women see through him?"

"Oh, he's smooth. Cultured. He's from old money, though his father lost most of it. Grant made a lot of it back with land deals—some above-board, some not." Jack smiled grimly. "Investors, politicians, society matrons...hell, just about everyone...believes whatever Grant wants them to believe. And he goes after his women with every-thing he has. He rents jets, flies them around the world on dates, writes love poems. While he was dating Sarah, he even bought himself puppies to raise, just to impress her. Grant, with puppies. Ha."

Connor was beginning to feel sick.

"He does real well in the romance department until he marries a woman," Jack explained. "Then he changes—like Dr. Jekyll and Mr. Hyde. He starts feeling like he owns her. When I heard Sarah was marrying him, I wanted to warn her. I hated for anyone else to go through what my sister had. Besides, I liked Sarah the couple of times we met." He paused and smiled in pleasant contemplation. "We just kind of...clicked, you know?"

"Clicked?" repeated Connor ominously, not particularly liking Jack's smile at the moment.

He raised a brow, as if surprised by Connor's tone. "Friend-wise, I mean." Leaning forward, he studied Connor with a renewed interest. "If you don't mind my asking, what's *your* relationship with her?"

"I mind you asking."

Jack sat back, one end of his mouth kicking up in a grin.

Connor's lips thinned in annoyance. "Did you warn her about Tierney, or not?"

"I tried. She'd already left for Colorado, though, and I didn't know how to contact her. So, I showed up at the wedding."

"But you were too late," Connor guessed.

"Too late to talk to her, yeah. By the time I got there, the ceremony had already started. An odd thing happened, though. After Grant put the ring on her finger and the minister was about to pronounce them man and wife, Sarah held up her hands and said, 'Wait. I'm not ready to do this.'"

Connor stared at him, his heart slowing to a near standstill. "She stopped the ceremony?"

Jack nodded. "She apologized to Grant, gave him back his ring and walked out."

The breath left Connor's body and he couldn't seem to draw another. "She didn't marry him?"

"Not then. She may have later, I suppose."

"You don't know whether or not she married him?" he shouted, barely refraining from grabbing him again and shaking his teeth loose.

"If you give me a damn minute, I'll tell you what happened!" Jack yelled.

The men glared at each other as Connor's sudden hope warred with confusion. She'd told him she was married, and that she loved her husband. She *had* to have married Tierney.

Jack took another swig of water and wiped his

forearm across his mouth. "He followed her to a room at the back of the chapel. I recognized the look on his face. There was trouble brewing. So, I went along, too. I didn't want to see Sarah get hurt. He tried to pressure her into going through with the ceremony. I was afraid he might succeed. I probably should have waited until he'd cooled down some, but I didn't want to lose my chance to warn Sarah. I asked if he'd told her about his first two wives." His gaze locked with Connor's. "He hadn't. She didn't know he'd ever been married."

"How did she take the news?"

"She wasn't too happy. He was furious that I'd brought it up. She asked me if I'd take her home, and I said I would. Grant went berserk. He accused me of trying to take her away from him. He came at me, we fought, and he drew a gun."

"He carried a gun on his wedding day?"

"Always. He makes some powerful enemies in his line of work. Anyway, he shot me. The first bullet grazed my face. The second hit my shoulder. I guess I lost consciousness. The last thing I remember was Grant running out of the door after Sarah, yelling that she belonged to him."

"My God." Pieces of the puzzle began to fall into place. "No wonder she had nightmares about being chased."

"Someone called the police. They apprehended Grant on a downtown street. Sarah must have eluded him—maybe cut through a shop or a side street. I'm assuming she was then hit by Annie Tompkins's car. I found out later we were both admitted to the same hospital at the same time."

Connor thought back to the story Sarah had told

him—about waking up in the hospital with total amnesia and no identification on her. He understood now why she hadn't been carrying a purse, but... "Wasn't she wearing a bridal gown?"

"Nope. Some light-colored suit, if I remember right."

The realization hit him, then. If she hadn't married Tierney that day, *she couldn't have married him at all.* Annie had brought her straight home to Sugar Falls from the hospital.

"I kept waiting for Sarah to call me and ask how I was recuperating," Jack remarked. "She never did. I assumed she'd either gone back to Grant and was afraid to call me, or that she'd taken off for parts unknown to get away from him."

"Why didn't *he* look for her, or file a missing-persons report?"

"He's got a history of women running away from him. It's nothing new. And, until a few days ago, he's been in jail. Assault with a deadly weapon."

Sarah couldn't have married him. The knowledge pulsed through Connor with every beat of his heart. Struggling to understand the situation entirely—to be sure he wasn't jumping to a false conclusion—he questioned, "So then, why did you start looking for her?"

"Sarah's Aunt Martha called Grant's mother, who still lives next door to me. When she mentioned to me that Sarah's aunt hadn't heard from her since the wedding, I got worried and started checking around for her."

"But you told Annie her name might be Sarah

Myers Tierney. If she'd called off the wedding, why would she have Tierney's name?"

"For all I know, she could have changed her mind and married Tierney while he was in jail. You did say she went back to him, right?"

"Today. A few hours ago." Angry at himself for not stopping her, Connor released a long, hard breath, cursed himself and tried to make sense of the situation. "She told me she was married to him, but she can't be. She's been here, in Sugar Falls, since the accident."

And she hadn't remembered Tierney's existence until last night. Yet, she'd said she loved him. Just remembering it pierced him with fresh pain. Had she gone back to Tierney with the intention of marrying him? He couldn't stand the thought. "Why the hell did she go back to him?" he blurted in frustration.

"I know this is hard to accept, Doc, but some women won't leave a relationship, no matter how bad it gets."

He couldn't believe that of Sarah. She had too much spirit to walk back into an abusive relationship; too much vitality, inner strength and self-esteem.

With a bemused shake of his shaggy blond head, Jack stated, "It took my sister two hellish years to wise up. She insisted she was in love."

Connor shut his eyes. *"Do you love him?"* he'd asked Sarah. *"Yes."*

But damn it, he didn't believe her. When he'd gazed into her eyes, he'd seen her love...*for him.* When they'd shared long, hot kisses and passionate lovemaking, he'd felt her love...*for him.* It could have been gratitude, fondness or lust, but his heart kept telling him that it had been love.

Why, then, had she returned to a man from whom she'd run in terror?

A possibility struck Connor. Maybe she hadn't remembered the ugly scene at the chapel. Maybe she'd pieced together incomplete memories and had come up with the wrong picture.

He could see how that might have happened.

She'd remembered a man pushing a wedding band onto her finger. She'd been told by her aunt that she was married to Grant Tierney. Sarah would have taken that as proof that she was, in fact, married. She would have felt a duty to do the honorable thing—to return to her husband and give her marriage a chance.

Which meant she now believed Grant Tierney to be her husband. She wouldn't know his true nature. She wouldn't know that the wrong word could fuel his rage. She might attempt to speak honestly with him. She might admit that she'd lost her virginity to another man.

Tierney would kill her. He'd surely kill her.

A cold fist squeezed Connor's heart. "Do you know where Tierney lives?"

"Yeah, but—"

"Tell me."

Jack frowned and slanted him a questioning glance. "Why?"

"I've got to get Sarah out of there."

"Are you crazy? He'll kill you, man. And you'll only make things worse for Sarah if she wants to stay. She walked back into the relationship with her eyes wide open this time. She saw him shoot me in a jealous rage, yet she still went back to him. As much as I hate it, there's nothing we can do until she's had enough."

"I don't believe she remembers him."

Jack's frown deepened. "What do you mean?"

"Amnesia. She's had amnesia. Memories have started coming back, and yesterday, she told me she remembered her husband. After hearing your story, though, I don't believe she remembers what happened at the chapel...or she wouldn't have gone back to him."

"You never know with women."

Connor leveled a hard, warning stare at Jack. "With Sarah, *I know.*"

THE EXCLUSIVE DENVER neighborhood looked vaguely familiar to Sarah from the back seat of the cab as it motored along quiet, tree-lined streets, past the clubhouse, tennis courts and swimming pool. She sat perfectly still with her hands clenched in her lap, trying to reason away the fear.

The cab turned into a sloped driveway, then pulled to a halt in front of sprawling, white-brick trilevel. The driver turned to Sarah, who remained frozen in the back seat. "This is the place, right?"

She barely heard him. Her fear had intensified. "Stay here," she instructed. "Wait for me. I may need to leave soon."

"Take all the time you want. It's your dollar."

She murmured her thanks, then ventured nervously toward the house. She remembered this place, with its manicured gardens, flowering trees and huge evergreens. She'd been happy and impressed when she'd first seen it. Why, then, were her knees shaking as she climbed the front steps?

Bracing herself as best she could, she rang the bell.

The glossy wooden door opened, and Grant Tierney stood there in a casual navy blazer, gray silk shirt and European-style trousers. With his crystal-blue eyes, ebony hair and aristocratic bearing, he could have stepped from the pages of a men's fashion journal or a celebrity life-style magazine.

"Sarah." A smile warmed his face and a sheen sprang to his eyes. "You've come back to me." With hands on her arms, he drew her into the house. "I've missed you so much. You have no idea what it did to me to hear your voice on that recorder, telling me you were coming home." He pulled her against him in a tight embrace.

The crisp scent of his cologne, the wiry feel of his body, the brush of his stiffly styled hair against her temple, brought back more memories of times they'd spent together. Specifically, the days before their wedding.

She'd been having doubts, she remembered suddenly. His embraces, his gazes, his possessive whispers, had begun to seem too cloying. She'd tried to chalk up the feeling to prewedding jitters.

She realized now, it had been much more than that. She hadn't really loved him. She'd been dazzled by his style, his charm and his extravagant attentions, but she hadn't known what it meant to really fall in love.

She did now. She'd fallen hard for Connor.

"I'm sorry, Grant." She eased back from his embrace, conscious of the fear that kept her from relaxing in his presence. She felt as if she had to watch every word she said; as if she might somehow displease him. "This is hard for me. I've been away for so long. So much has happened."

"I thought you'd left me. I nearly went out of my mind."

She stared at him in dismay. She couldn't possibly stay with him. Had she realized that after the wedding? Was that why she hadn't slept with him; why her virginity had remained intact? Of course, these questions were only a few of many. Why hadn't he filed a missing-persons report? Why hadn't he told Aunt Martha?

"Grant, we need to talk. I have so many questions."

"Of course we need to talk. Where were you? Why didn't you call, or visit me?"

"Visit you?" She frowned. An odd thing for a husband to ask a wife who's been missing for two months.

"You didn't know," he said with sudden realization. "You didn't know that they'd taken me, did you?" He stared at her with eyes that shone a little too brightly.

"Taken you?" The fear stirred within her. "Grant, what do you mean?"

"The police. They arrested me. I've been in jail for over two months. Oh, Sarah, I needed you so much." He wrapped his arms around her in another tight embrace.

And the memories clicked into place. All of them. Vivid, full-blown memories. An unvoiced sob lodged in her throat. He'd shot Jack! She'd stopped the wedding and asked Jack to take her home. And Grant had shot him!

"Can you believe they're blaming me for what happened?" he said, his smooth-shaven chin pressing against her ear. "A man attacks me at my own wedding, and they blame me. Thank heavens I've got good attorneys."

Speechless with horror, she replayed the gruesome finale of their wedding day. There'd been so much blood. She'd thought Jack had died.

But he hadn't. He'd called Annie's house yesterday, looking for her. Jack had survived! How could she have forgotten who he was?

"Let's talk over supper." Grant slid an arm around her and swept her along through a spacious living room decorated in white, chrome and glass. "I've made some of your favorites. We'll start with Crabmeat Jean Baptiste, like they serve at Broussard's. You loved that dish there, remember? You wore your blue velvet dress, and the diamond earrings I'd bought for you in Paris. You were the most beautiful woman in—"

"Grant, stop." She halted near the archway of an elegant dining room whose table had been set for two. The late-afternoon sun slanted in golden rays through the floor-to-ceiling windows, illuminating the beauty of the crystal, silver and fine china. "I'm sorry if you misunderstood my message on your recorder, but I haven't come back to you."

He drew his dark brows together in a frown.

"I've come to get the luggage I left here," she explained, "and my purse, if you still have it."

"Of course I have it. The luggage is still packed for our honeymoon. I'm ready to start that honeymoon now. I've waited long enough already. We're going to have a cozy night together, and then tomorrow we're flying to Hawaii for a couple of weeks to start our life together, as man and wife." Though his voice was gentle, the determined sparkle in his eyes chilled her.

"Grant, we're not married."

"And whose fault is that?" he asked softly. With a sense of shock, she realized that anger lurked beneath the congeniality in his gaze. "Tell me, Sarah. Whose fault?"

"Mine," she whispered, her fear growing. "I stopped the ceremony because I had doubts. They were valid doubts."

"You walked down that aisle. I put my ring on your finger. I don't care about legalities." He leaned closer and whispered, "You're mine."

She swallowed against rising panic. He was furious that she'd stopped the wedding. So furious that he intended to ignore the fact that she'd stopped it.

"But I don't love you." She backed a few steps away from him, into the living room and closer to the door. She had the cab waiting for her in the driveway. All she had to do was get to it. "Why would you want to be tied to a wife who doesn't love you?"

"Oh, you'll love me." He said it as if he could force her into it. "You made promises to me, Sarah, and you will keep them."

She clasped her hands behind her back to stop them from trembling and casually paced away from him, toward the front door. How could he have hidden this side of his personality from her so completely? "You can't threaten me into marrying you."

Taking two long strides, he caught her face in his hand. "You have already married me." His grip on her chin grew painful. "Tomorrow we'll sign whatever papers we need to complete the process."

"Let go of me," she ordered with all the authority she could command. She couldn't allow the fear to overcome her. She had to keep a calm head.

He lowered his hand from her face, but his nearness forced her to back against the foyer's wall. "I will never let go of you. You will always be mine. And tonight, I'll take what's mine."

She stared into his obsessed eyes and realized she was living her nightmare. He'd been chasing her through all those horrible nights…and now, he'd caught her.

"Let's make this a happy night, Sarah." His gaze roamed her face. "It should be the best night of our married lives. It can be, you know. You'll like it. I promise."

A shiver snaked down her spine.

He swooped in to kiss her. She turned her face. His mouth nudged her cheek. He laughed softly, as if she'd delighted him. "I know you're nervous. That's okay. It's only natural, for your first time." Fervently, he added, "I've waited so long for this. You will *not* deny me." He covered her mouth with his.

She had to do something before he forced her to a bedroom. He held her too tightly; she couldn't move. If only she could get him to loosen his hold…

"Grant," she gasped, twisting her head to evade his prying kiss, "this won't be my first time."

He stiffened as if he'd been stunned by a live wire.

"While I was gone," she confessed, "I fell in love. And we were...intimate."

Slowly, with a hissing of breath, he drew back from her. A chilling hardness descended over his face, and his eyes pierced her with crystal-blue coldness. "Then you're just like all the rest. Tainted. Dirty. Used."

She gaped at him. How could he possibly be the same man who had once clamored to please her? "I wouldn't put it quite like that," she replied in a trembling voice.

He slammed his fist into the wall. "Whore!"

That supplied the adrenaline rush she needed. Concentrating all her strength into one swift move, she jerked her knee up into his groin. *Thud.*

A startled look suffused his face. He gasped, paled and doubled over.

With her heart hammering, she pushed the door open and flew down the steps, into the golden sunglow of early evening.

As she looked back in abject fear, she ran solidly into a man's hard, broad chest. Strong arms clutched her, warm and steadying. "Sarah!" exclaimed the gruff, familiar voice. "Are you okay?"

Connor!

Her heart contracted with wild terror. "What are you doing here? You'll be killed!" She threw a panicked glance toward the door. "Get out of here, Connor. Now!" She pushed at his chest and batted at him wildly, trying to drive him backward, to force him to leave. "Go, go!" she cried through clenched teeth.

Flinching at her blows, he muttered an oath, grabbed her flailing arms and pulled her farther out into the yard, behind a huge, thick evergreen bush. "Shh. Sarah! Calm down." He gripped her arms and held her still. "Did he hurt you?"

"No, no." Her heart thudded with fear for him. "But he'll kill you if he sees you with me."

"Something sent you running from that house." Protective anger blazed in his beautiful eyes like golden-green fire, and a muscle throbbed in his jaw. "Tell me what it was. If he hurt you, Sarah I swear I'll—"

"Connor!" She caught his face between her hands, her desperation growing. "Please, please listen. He didn't hurt me. I just remembered…oh, God, I remembered—" a shudder went through her "—he shot Jack."

He pulled her to him in a hard, rocking hug, whispering into her hair, "I know, sweetheart, I know."

"You *know?*" She pulled back and glared at him through the lengthening shadows of the encroaching twilight. "Then why did you come here? Are you crazy? Do you want to die?"

"I came to get you."

"I can't leave with you! If he sees us together, he'll get his gun. He'll kill you!" A sob escaped her. "I couldn't bear it. I'd rather die—"

Connor cut off her cry with a kiss. Her mouth opened beneath his and they clung together in sweet desperation. She knew, then. She knew that he needed her as much as she needed him.

"Hellfire!" exclaimed a deep, masculine whisper behind them, jarring them apart. "I get shot for saying I'll drive her home, and you're necking with her in the bushes."

"Damn it, Jack," Connor cursed, "you nearly gave me a heart attack."

"Jack!" Sarah gazed at him in astonishment, bewildered by how and why he was here. "Oh, Jack..." She left Connor's arms and went into his as tears welled up in her eyes. "I'm so sorry for getting you shot."

"Just a couple of flesh wounds. Gives me character."

"Your poor face!"

"Yeah, he's still too pretty," Connor muttered wryly. "Let's get the hell out of here before Tierney remedies that." He pulled Sarah to his side with an arm insistently around her.

"You two go on," she argued. "I'll take the cab I have waiting. I don't want to risk having Grant see me with you."

A shadow fell across the lawn before them. The shadow of a man.

Grant Tierney stepped into their path. Gone from his face was every trace of reason, leaving only stark coldness. "You're a little too late for that."

Sarah froze in terror at Connor's side.

"I sent the cab away," Grant informed with cultured gentility. "When I didn't find you in it, Sarah, I couldn't imagine where you were. In the bushes, I see. With a man. Why doesn't that surprise me?"

Connor growled and surged toward him.

Sarah clutched his arm fiercely, desperate to hold him back. She'd noticed that Grant had reached into his sport jacket. She'd seen him reach that way before...*when he'd shot Jack.* Her mouth dry with terror, she whispered, "He has a gun."

Connor shoved her behind him and tried to hold her there as he glowered at Grant. "I have a matter to discuss with you," he said curtly, "but I want her out of here first."

Grant ignored what he'd said and gazed past him to Sarah. "He's the one, isn't he?" he asked her. "The one you fell in love with. The one you *did it* with."

Connor lunged at him, toppling him backward. Jack leaped from the shadows, shoved Sarah to the ground and sprawled across her to keep her down. She sobbed and struggled to break free, wanting to shield Connor from danger. She fully expected to hear a gunshot at any moment.

The fight, however, ended as quickly as it had begun. Connor dug his knee into Grant's back, twisted his arms behind him and pushed his face down into the grass. "Don't you ever, *ever*, talk to Sarah that way," he thundered between clenched teeth, wrenching Grant's arms with every inflection. "Don't you touch her, don't you call her, don't you come anywhere near her, or I'll kill you. Do you understand that?"

Grant grunted an acknowledgement.

Jack, meanwhile, released his hold on Sarah and lumbered to his feet. She saw him bend to pick up an object from the grass.

A gun.

A shudder went through her.

Jack sauntered to a motorcycle in the driveway and dropped the gun into a pouch. Strolling back with a cell phone, he called the police. "I'll take over from here, Doc," he drawled, slipping the phone into a pocket inside his leather vest. "It would give me the greatest of pleasure."

Sarah watched the men exchange places and trade wry quips, although Connor's gaze continued to simmer with anger as he looked down at their captive. How in the world, she wondered, had Connor ever hooked up with Jack?

After his fight, looking tough and exquisitely virile with a sheen of sweat glinting on his muscled forearms and sun-darkened face, a lock of his tawny hair falling forward over one eye, Connor strode to Sarah, extended a strong hand and helped her up.

"Were you hurt?" He brushed the grass off her skirt and vest, touching her here and there in a quick, expert check for injuries. "You took one hell of a tackle."

With a shaky laugh, she stopped him from sweeping her skirt aside to examine her knees. "I'm fine, Doc. I swear it."

Tenderness warmed his gaze as he met her smile. "Let's wait in my car until the police get here."

Gratefully she accepted his strong arm around her waist as they walked to the Jaguar. She settled against his lean, muscular body with a pleasing familiarity. She wanted him nearer still. She wanted to touch him, feel him, kiss him. Love him.

"The wedding's off, Sarah," Grant hollered from where Jack held him captive, his voice somewhat muffled by the grass. "You blew it. I can't marry you now."

She was surprised to hear his voice—she'd almost forgotten he existed—and her heart beat a happy little tattoo at the news. Never had a rejection filled her with such relief.

Grant then chided Connor in a tone of scathing mockery, "You can have her, mister!"

Connor stiffened, his fists clenched and his bottom lip curled. Sarah laid a gentling hand on his arm. "It's actually not too bad a suggestion...is it?"

He turned his warrior stare toward her, and within seconds, it softened and warmed. His lips even curved into the start of a smile. "Only if it's true," he replied hoarsely, his gaze pressing into hers. "Can I have her?"

Her breath caught in her throat. She loved him so much! "I don't see why not. I know now that I'm not married. I don't understand how I could have forgotten that I'd walked out of the chapel, but—"

Connor turned her against the car and kissed her. She wrapped her arms around his neck and melted against him. He closed his eyes and reveled in the taste of her. When the need and the longing to make love to her again grew too intense, he lifted his head to catch his breath and remind himself of where he was.

Heaven, he realized, gazing deeply into the eyes he'd thought he'd never see again. He had plunged into hell, and had somehow ended up in heaven. "What about that other thing Tierney said," he whispered, "when he asked if you were in love with me? I didn't hear your answer."

The sweetest, warmest tenderness prompted her

smile. "I fell in love with you the first time you looked into my eyes. I think it was with one of those scope lights."

He smiled, feeling the happiness take root deep within him. "I fell in love with you," he disclosed, "the first time you said 'Ahhh.'" He pressed a kiss to her nose. "And the second time." He rained kisses along her eyelids. "And the third." He nipped and tugged at her mouth, the heat in him growing serious. "I can't wait until the fourth."

They met in a hot, yearning kiss— one that only made their need for each other more urgent.

"I love you, Sarah," he swore. "You're a part of me that I'd die without. I want you in my life, in my bed. Marry me."

"Okay," she breathed.

They lost themselves in each other.

"Aw, jeez," Jack muttered, coming up behind them, "you two can really pick your places. I'll bet you didn't even realize that half-a-dozen police cars just drove off with their sirens blaring."

Separating only as far as necessary, Connor and Sarah cast Jack a slightly dazed glance.

"Your point?" asked Connor.

Jack gave a rueful laugh. "The police took Tierney. I guess I'll be going down to the station to answer some questions, then heading out on the open road. Can't say it hasn't been interesting."

Connor grasped his hand warmly, patted his back and thanked him. Sarah hugged him, swore eternal gratitude and made him promise to visit.

He turned toward his motorcycle, keys in hand, then pivoted back. "Oh, by the way, Doc..."

"Yeah?" replied Connor.

"Actually, I was talking to Sarah."

Connor raised a quizzical brow. "Did you call her 'Doc'?"

Sarah bit her lip to stifle a smile as more memories fluttered back to her.

"Didn't she tell you?" Jack asked, blatantly enjoying himself. "She's a pet psychologist. An animal behaviorist. A critter shrink. Ph.D."

With a pleased twist of his mouth, Connor tilted his head and stared at her, duly impressed. "Now why doesn't that surprise me?"

"Sure you won't mind?" she teased. "We'll be Dr. and Dr. Wade."

They laughed. He kissed her—just a brief caress of their lips—but their gazes held and grew tender again.

Jack shook his head in mock censure. "Before you two get all lovey-dovey, I just wanted to tell Dr. Sarah, here, that my alligator is doing much better since the last time we talked about him."

"Great!" She regarded him with bright interest. "Has he stopped chasing cars?"

"No, but we've closed the beach to traffic. Problem solved."

She poked her tongue against her cheek. They exchanged droll looks. Jack lifted a hand in goodbye and sauntered toward his bike.

"Hey, Jack," Connor called out. "Just out of curiosity, what do *you* do for a living?"

Swinging his leg over the huge black-and-chrome Harley, he settled onto the leather seat and pulled the helmet down on his shaggy blond head. Just before he cranked up the engine, he replied, "Orthopedic surgery."

With a flash of a smile, he lowered the shield of his helmet and blasted off down the drive.

Connor turned a stunned look on Sarah. "He's a *surgeon?*"

She cocked her head. Her eyes sparkled merrily at him. "Didn't I mention that?"

He dragged her to him with playful sternness. "No, ma'am. I don't believe you did." He ran his hands down her back and around to her hips, molding her body intimately to his. "There's quite a few things you forgot to mention."

Thoroughly distracted by the feel of his muscle-hard body against hers and the seduction of his heated stare, she barely managed to whisper, "Like what?"

"Like your full, real name." He brushed his mouth in a lingering path across hers, inciting a riot of sensual reaction in her. "Where you're from," he whispered against her ear before swirling his tongue inside it. "How long I have to wait before I'm inside you again."

She answered his last question first—to his full satisfaction—with action rather than words.

They'd have a lifetime to fill in the less important details.

If you enjoyed what you just read,
then we've got an offer you can't resist!

Take 2 bestselling love stories FREE!

Plus get a FREE surprise gift!

COMING NEXT MONTH

#729 IT TAKES A HERO Gina Wilkins
Bachelor Auction

Romance author Kristin Cole didn't need a man—she needed a
hero! With writer's block staring her in the face, Kristin couldn't
resist bidding on gorgeous Perry Goodman, just for inspiration.
But Perry wasn't a one-night hero. He was holding out for a
"happily ever after"—one that included her....

#730 LOGAN'S WAY Lisa Ann Verge

Ambushed! That's how Dr. Logan Macallistair felt when his
peaceful retreat was invaded by a sexy redhead. The indomitable
Eugenia Van Saun, Ph.D.—botanist with an attitude—was using
his cabin for research? He'd been alone and he wanted to stay
that way. Still, looking at Ginny, he had a growing appreciation
for flowers, the birds and the bees...and who better to explore
them with?

#731 NOT IN MY BED! Kate Hoffmann
The Wrong Bed

Carrie Reynolds had only one weakness: Devlin Riley. The sexy
adventurer played the starring role in all Carrie's thoughts and
fantasies. When Carrie went on vacation, she wasn't particularly
surprised that Devlin showed up while she slept, stroking her,
seducing her.... Then she woke up—and discovered she wasn't
dreaming....

#732 FORBIDDEN Janelle Denison
Blaze

For years Detective Josh Marchiano had been in love with his
partner's wife. But now, Paige was a widow—and she was in
danger. Torn between guilt and desire, Josh vowed to protect her
at all costs. Little did he guess that he'd have to stay by her side
all day...and in her bed all night!